CATCH ME

SPRING HILL BLUES

BOOK TWO

By
E. M. MOORE

This book is a work of fiction. Names, characters, places, and incidents are the product of the author's imagination or are used fictitiously. Any resemblance to actual events, or persons, living or dead, is coincidental.

Copyright © 2019 by E. M. Moore. All rights reserved, including the right to reproduce, distribute, or transmit in any form or by any means. For information regarding subsidiary rights, please contact E. M. Moore at emmoorewrites@hotmail.com.

Manufactured in the United States of America
First Edition December 2019

Cover by 2nd Life Designs

Also By E. M. Moore

The Heights Crew Series

Uppercut Princess

Arm Candy Warrior

The Ballers of Rockport High Series

Game On

Foul Line

At the Buzzer

Rockstars of Hollywood Hill

Rock On

Spring Hill Blue Series

Free Fall

Catch Me

Ravana Clan Vampires Series

Chosen By Darkness

Into the Darkness

Falling For Darkness

Surrender To Darkness

Ravana Clan Legacy Series

A New Genesis

Tracking Fate

Cursed Gift

Veiled History

Fractured Vision

Chosen Destiny

Order of the Akasha Series

Stripped (Prequel)

Summoned By Magic

Tempted By Magic

Ravished By Magic

Indulged By Magic

Enraged By Magic

Her Alien Scouts Series

Kain Encounters

Kain Seduction

Rise of the Morphlings Series

Of Blood and Twisted Roots

Safe Haven Academy Series

A Sky So Dark

A Dawn So Quiet

Chronicles of Cas Series

Reawakened

Hidden

Power

Severed

Rogue

The Adams' Witch Series

Bound In Blood

Cursed In Love

Witchy Librarian Cozy Mystery Series

Wicked Witchcraft

One Wicked Sister

Wicked Cool

Wicked Wiccans

1

Sometime in the last minute or so, the dank, mold-infested hotel room faded away.

My eyes focus on a pair of blue-green irises staring straight back at me. By all measures, they're pretty. Exotic even, but what's inside is dark. Dangerous. Sasha is an evil mastermind dressed up like a showpiece.

Her lips turn into a smirk. She moves further into the hotel room, casting our surroundings a disgusted once-over before returning her attention to me. It's clear she would never be caught dead in a place like this. Not Sasha Pontine. "This was more fun than I thought." She laughs, the sound harsher than anything I've heard lately, and that's saying something since I've been begging on the streets for a week. "You were too easy to manipulate, Briar. I mean, I barely said anything over the messages, but you just took right off, telling me all your thoughts and feelings."

My mind races, thinking of everything I poured out, thinking of how the person on the other end of the screen had felt like a lifeline for so long. The whole time it was Sasha, laughing. My stomach threatens to expel again, but I won't give her the gratification of that. Of losing myself over her. I want to ask her what the hell she wants, but instead, my lips form the question, "Why?"

Slowly, she crosses her arms over her chest. "*Why* did I mess with you?" She shrugs. "It was fun. I was bored. You were there."

Her words repeat in my head over and over. There's a special place in hell for people like Sasha. She's even worse than I imagined. She's not just self-centered and cruel, she gets off on being mean. After we stare one another down for a moment, I say, "What are you doing here? Just throwing it in my face that I never really had a friend?"

"Now that would be too easy." Her eyes flash. "No, I have more planned. You see, you really screwed up the thing Reid and I had going."

My eyes go out of focus as a sharp stab hits my

chest. She said his name. His name on her lips is so, so wrong.

Reid...

My heart clutches his name, not wanting to let it go. I've tried not to think about him the whole time I've been gone. I've tried not to think about anyone from home. There's too much there.

She pierces me with a look, and I realize the painful groan I hear in my ears is actually me, filling the hotel room with my pain. It's the sound I make when I replay what happened to Reid out on that football field. My mind begs me to ask her how he is, but at the same time, I won't give her the satisfaction. I also know that whatever comes out of her mouth is most likely a lie.

"Get over yourself," she snaps. "He's a good lay, but not *that* good."

My gaze narrows. Doesn't she know it's not about that? I take her in. Her perfect hair, her designer outfit. To her, it's probably all about that. In that moment, I feel a little sorry for her. A little. She doesn't know what love is—and that's tragic.

The doorknob turns and the barrier between me and my real life pushes open once more. Sasha and I immediately turn that way. I back up, but the first thing out of Sasha's mouth is, "Took you long enough."

"Sorry, babe. I got busy."

She rolls her eyes.

The backs of my legs hit the bed, and I take a seat. The bed squeaks, causing the newcomer to look over. "So, this is her?"

"Yeah," Sasha says, not sparing me a glance. She grabs his shirt and yanks him toward her. Their lips collide until they fall into a raucous wrestling match that looks like it's about who can bite the other's face off first. I turn away.

"Don't forget what you promised me," a husky voice says, emerging from the sucking noises.

"I always come through," Sasha says, her voice flipping from bitch to vixen in a heartbeat.

They start making out again, so I get up and walk toward the door. I'm not staying here. I don't know where I'm going, but my heart hurts. It's heavy in my chest. The owner of the hotel has a phone in the office. Maybe I should make that call, the one I told myself I wouldn't make after I'd wake in sweats from a night filled with dreams about home. I told myself I couldn't take the pain of returning, but I can't take the pain of being away either.

A hand comes around my midsection, clamping down. "No, you don't."

The hand pushes back, sending me stumbling

toward the bed. Once again, the mattress catches my knees, and I plop back on the bed. Sasha moves in front of me, making me look up to face her. She runs a finger under her bottom lip, fixing the smear of lipstick. "Here's what's going to happen, Briar. I get what I want. It occurred to me that that photo I have of you with your tiny little tit wouldn't do much, but I had the thought that I could do so much better. So, I brought *him* here to do just that."

The new guy starts to take his shirt off. He's got an athletic body built for sports. My eyes stay trained on his face, and that's when it hits me. I know this guy. I've seen him before. "You," I say.

He smiles. We all know what I'm talking about, but none of us voice it aloud. My heart rips again, thinking about the tackle that took Reid down. Like it just happened, I see a guy run back to the sidelines with a smirk on his face. It's this guy. I'm sure of it.

Sasha pulls her pink glittery cell phone out. "Alright, let's get started."

I turn toward her, unsure of what she's even talking about. The guy eases the button on his jeans and lowers his zipper. Panic claws at my throat as Sasha starts snapping pictures. "What are you doing?"

"Making your life miserable. If you think Reid will want you again after this..."

Sasha's accomplice takes my hand and puts them on the waistband of his jeans. I'm too numb to do anything at first, but once he holds them there, I pull out of his grip. "Stop."

"I'm not going to do anything to you, babe," the guy says, a spark of mischief in his eyes. "We're just going to take some pictures."

I try to get up, to push past him, but he uses his weight to push me back onto the bed. Following after me, he lands with his knee at the apex of my thighs and my hands pinned above my head.

"I wanted her clothes off before we had any bed pics," Sasha snaps.

"She fought back. What did you want me to do?"

I try to wiggle out of his grip. "You two are crazy." I pull my leg up to try to push him off, but all he does is sink more of his body weight onto me.

"Shit, I'm getting hard," he says, humor lacing his voice. "I like it rough, Sasha. You better watch out."

"Just pull her shirt up. I need something incriminating. When Reid sees that she left him just to hook up with other guys, he'll drop her so damn fast."

He holds my hands over my head and reaches down with his other. Slowly, he lifts my shirt up, and when his fingers touch my bare skin, my body ices over.

In the next instant, I thrash, looking for any way to get this guy off me.

"Hold her down," Sasha screeches.

"She's stronger than she looks."

He goes up on his knees to try to pin me down harder, but he's made a fatal mistake. I bring my knee up, and it connects with his balls.

He groans. "Fuck. Bitch!"

I push him off me and move toward the door, but it careens open the second I start for it. My eyes try to adjust to the new light in the room, and at first, all I see is a hulking figure filling the doorway, but when the figure steps in, I almost collapse in relief.

"Briar!"

"Lex!"

He makes it to me in three strides and holds me to his side. His body is warm, vibrating underneath my touch with barely concealed anger as he takes the scene in. "What the fuck?"

I shake in his arms, and he holds me closer, stepping in front of me so he shields my body.

Sasha has the good sense to look a little scared. Her eyes round for a fraction of a second, but then her facade clicks into place. "Really?" she asks, looking over at the guy who's still clutching his balls protectively.

"Fuck you," he groans. "That fucking hurt."

"You're about to hurt a lot fucking worse." Lex takes a step toward his sprawled body on the bed, but hesitates. I can tell he doesn't want to let go of me, and right now, I don't want to let him go either. I'm cracking into pieces at his side.

"Whatever," Sasha says, yanking on his arm to help him off the bed. "Let's get the fuck out of here."

Lex moves in front of the door, taking me with him. "I don't think so. The police are on their way. They want to talk to you about a picture you have on your phone."

Sasha's face colors. She moves her phone in front of her face and taps the screen a few times. It takes me a second to realize she's deleting the pictures she's just took.

"It doesn't matter if you delete it," Lex says, gripping my forearm. "They've already seen it. They know you have it."

"There are other pictures!" I move forward and snatch her cell out of her hand. She gives it up willingly and when I look through her photo album, I realize why. She's deleted all the ones she's just taken.

Now it's my word against theirs.

I throw her phone back at her. It hits her chest, past her outstretched hands, and falls to the ground.

Sasha glares at it between her feet and then moves her wicked gaze to look me in the eyes. "You think that's the only thing I had planned. You're wrong."

Sirens echo behind us. I know I should be scared that the police will be here soon and the fact that I'm a runaway and the photo and the piece of shit guy across from me who looks like he's about to crap himself, but I'm caught by the lifelessness in Sasha's eyes.

She truly means what she says. She has it out for us, and she's not going to stop until she gets it.

2

I don't leave Lex's side. His strong arms never let me go as he wades us through police questioning. I'm relieved when her guy leaves, if only because I don't have to look at his face anymore. Not only did he hurt Reid, but he put his slimy hands on me.

A half an hour later, after her parents show up, Sasha's led to a police car and is put in the back. Without handcuffs, unfortunately. If the looks from her parents could kill, though. Damn. Instead of looking at Lex and I that way, they should be turning around and piercing their daughter with that same hate-filled glare. Maybe it would teach her a few things.

Relief floods me when the police leave, leaving Lex

and I alone in the hotel room. I blink after the retreating red and blue lights, disbelieving. I thought for sure they were going to ask me about running away, or what we were all doing there, but the whole thing was about Sasha and the picture she had of me on her phone.

As soon as we're by ourselves, Lex turns my way. "Are you okay? What were they doing?" His hands move up to cup my face. "God, I've been crawling out of my skin, Briar."

The intensity in his brown eyes doesn't throw me. He's looked at me like that for a while now. I grab his hands and curl my fingers around them, holding him in place. "R-reid?"

He closes his eyes and breathes out. "He's okay. Severe concussion. Lucky Number Seven didn't even break a bone."

"But I heard a crack."

"We all did. That was his helmet."

"He's...he's okay?" My mouth wobbles.

Lex swears and pulls me to him. He wraps me in one of his big hugs and holds me there. "He's okay. He's fine. He's pissed off he can't be here right now, but his mom's watching him like a hawk." He kisses the top of my head. "I should probably call him."

I push away from him. "No. No, you can't do that."

Questions burn through his eyes. My throat constricts. What I've done hurls into me with a force of a wrecking ball. I left Reid when he needed me. I abandoned him. He's not going to want to hear from me.

"He wants to know how you are. He's been worried sick. We all have."

The room spins. I think about the conversation I had with Jules. It seems like it happened a hell of a lot longer than a week ago. Did I really ask her if it was better to have not loved Brady? I look up at Lex with spiked lashes. "There's something wrong with me."

"There's nothing wrong with you, Briar. Jules said you were in shock. We didn't know if you had a panic attack. We didn't know where you went or what happened to you."

"I ran away."

"I know, baby. I know."

He clasps my face again and pulls me to his chest. His even breaths help soothe me, but a hatred so deep sinks inside myself. I'm not any better than Sasha. I abandoned my friends. I abandoned the guy I love because what? Because I was too chicken to face what was going to happen next? That's low. That's despicable.

We stay standing, hugging one another, while a spiral of self-loathing churns inside me. Lex does his best to comfort me. Eventually, he moves me to the bed and holds me, his arms like tight bands. He kisses my temple. "I need you to tell me what Sasha and Richards were doing here?"

"Richards?"

A growl starts in Lex's chest, rumbling my face. "The fucker who hit Reid."

I close my eyes. I knew I was right. I knew that's who he was.

"How did you find me?"

Lex's muscles lock. I'm testing his patience. If he were Reid, he'd never let me get away with asking questions without answering his first, but Lex takes a deep breath and says, "It turns out Cade's fuck buddy is good for something. She checked Sasha's phone during practice and saw the messages between you and Ezra. We didn't know if Sasha actually knew anything except for the fact that she's been acting cagey and was the only other person who seemed to know you were missing. We told everyone you went to visit your grandparents for a little while." He squeezes me tighter. "I got here as soon as I could after calling the cops. The Hayley girl overheard Sasha saying she was going to meet someone at a hotel, so I knew she'd be here. I had to tell them about the picture, Briar. I'm so sorry. It's the only thing we have on Sasha right now."

I swallow. "Sasha is Ezra."

"I put that together." His fingers dig into me. "I'm sorry."

I blow out a breath. "I don't know why I messaged him. I didn't actually want him. I—"

"Shh," he says, rubbing his thumb over my cheek. "It's okay."

I wish it were. I wish everything could just go back to before Reid got hurt and before I decided to run away again. After a few minutes of scolding myself, I ask, "Where's Cade?"

"With Reid. Someone had to keep him there. Concussion or not, he was determined to come."

My heart breaks all over again. The now familiar selfish feeling hits me, accompanied by a need to hurt myself as much as these guys probably hate me. Just imagining Reid dealing with having a concussion and not knowing what happened to me makes every nerve ending in my body flare in regret. "Why are you here, Lex?"

He pulls away. Hurt darkens his eyes. "To help you."

"I've been so awful."

"You're hurting. There's a difference."

I shake my head. "Reid hates me."

"Reid…" His nostrils flare. "Fuck it. Reid loves you,

Briar. He's desperate to hear from you." He fishes for his phone again, but I pull away. "Don't do this," he says. "Haven't you learned by now that running away isn't the answer? You feel bad for running away and your answer to that is running even further away?" He shakes his head. "Briar, talk to him. Talk to us. All of us. We're scared. We're hurt. We want you back. *I* want you back."

His hand curls into me, giving me the strength I need. He hands me his phone. The screen lights up. I see missed calls and texts. One comes in while the phone is in my hand. **What's happening??? I swear to God, motherfucker, answer your goddamn phone.**

It's from Reid. Tears fracture my vision. I can picture him saying this, or watching his fingers fly over the on-screen keyboard right before he sends the message. A yearning builds inside me. I don't have any excuses for these guys. I can't tell them a reason why I ran away again because it all seems so dumb now that I'm here with Lex. It's never when I'm with other people that's the problem. It's when I'm by myself. It's when I'm lost in my own head. I can't even trust myself.

That is a scary ass feeling.

I take the phone from his grip and hit his Contacts

button. Scrolling, I stop when I see Reid and press the green phone to connect the call. The phone barely rings when the other end picks up. "Christ, Lex! What the fuck is happening?"

The sound of his voice eats away at me. I try to say, "Hi," but it comes out as a choked gasp. Then, the sobs come.

"Briar," he says. My name on his lips is like a promise. "Baby, baby, it's okay."

The nicer he is to me, the more I break down. I know I should be asking him a ton of questions. How is he? Is he hurt? Can I do anything for him? But even now, I can't get my body to cooperate.

"Give the phone to Lex, baby."

I hand it over, resting my head on Lex's chest again. His hand rubs up and down my arm. "She's okay."

"The hell she is! She's crying!"

"She's worried we all hate her."

A growl rips through the phone. His voice is tinny and low, but I can still hear it, anyway. "Tell her—."

"I've told her, Reid. She just needs a moment, I think. Sasha was here. The police took her. Richards was here too. I can't get out of her what they were doing."

"Bring her to me."

My body locks up, and Lex notices. He pulls away to look in my eyes. He hesitates with his answer, and in that span of time, Reid hangs up on him like it's already a done deal.

"We can be in Spring Hill in thirty minutes," Lex says.

"Is that my only option?" I ask, rubbing at my eyes, trying to halt the flow of tears.

We catch each other's gazes, and there are unspoken words between us. Words I think Lex is trying to convey rather than say. And to me, he's saying he'll do whatever I want. He'll stay here with me, if I want. He'll drive me to Spring Hill, if I want. Whatever I want, he'll do.

I also know that staying here will only delay the inevitable now. If I don't go to Spring Hill, Reid will come for me. I'm only prolonging the difficult conversation that lies ahead. The one where I hate myself more than anyone I've ever hated before.

Lex sees when I've made my decision, and I swear a little light dies from his eyes. "I'll take you to him."

3

*R*ight before we leave the hotel, Lex pays the balance I owe on the room. He forces me to call my parents on the way to Reid's. Mom sounds relieved, but curt. I guess they've already been through this with me. They started to think I was okay, and then bam, I leave again. I can't get mad at her for her attitude toward me. After she makes sure I'm okay, she asks to talk to whoever's with me, so I give the phone to Lex. He pulls the car over on the side of the highway to talk to her. I can't hear everything that's said, but I get the gist. She wants me home.

After he hangs up, he glances over at me, lips thin, "We'll have to make this visit short."

"She's mad," I say distractedly, peering out the window. "She has every reason to be."

"They ended their vacation early when they heard you ran away again."

I cringe. I have a lot of making up to do, *if* I can even make up for all the shit I've done. "I'll probably be grounded for the rest of my life."

"At least until you go to college."

The rest of the way to Reid's house, Lex explains that he, Cade, and Reid came up with the cover story about me visiting my grandparents. No one knows I ran away again except the ones closest to me, and Sasha, of course. I don't know how they got my parents to agree to the story instead of just calling the police, but here I am, being brought back to everything I ran away from and wondering why the need hit me so hard in the first place.

When I close my eyes, I still see Reid's still form in the hospital bed. The panic creeps up that maybe he isn't okay. Maybe he's destined to end up like Brady, and then what?

I don't know how I can explain it to everyone else because it seems so backwards.

The closer we get to Reid's house, the antsier I get. "Who all is there?"

"Probably everyone."

"Everyone?"

"Cade, Jules. Reid's parents."

"They're probably pissed at me too."

"No one's pissed at you."

I rub my eyes after they start to itch. He's lying. Lex would do anything to keep me safe. I stare at his profile while he urges the car forward. We've been in this exact place, except the car wasn't moving then. He did what I wanted, so I could feel better, even at the detriment to himself. The veins stick out on his arms as he hangs a left. He's locked up, rigid, like he's trying to contain shit inside. He might not even know he's doing it, but he is. "You've always been so good to me, Lex."

He blinks, then turns toward me for a brief second before watching the road again. "I'd do anything for you, Briar."

My heart beats painfully in my chest. When I look up, I notice he's pulled into Reid's driveway. The sun is setting, and the porch light is already on like a beacon. Lex throws his door open first, and I get out slowly. I look up at the sky for a second, asking Brady what the hell I've been doing for the past few months. He doesn't answer. He never does.

We walk past Cade's and Jules's car, parked just in front of the door. Everything in me is telling me to run away, but that instinct—that urge to run until I don't want to look back—has never done anything good for me. I don't even know where I got it from. It's like a disease. They should call it Houdini-itis because all I want is to escape.

A hand at my back keeps me moving forward. "They're going to be excited to see you," he says. He sounds like he means it, but I'm still wary.

With that, the front door opens. Mrs. Parker steps out, her hands to her mouth. She jogs down the steps and throws her arms around me. "Oh Briar. I've been as worried as if you were my own."

She squeezes me, not letting up, but then, Mr. Parker is there. He claps me on the back until Jules is in front of my face. Tears track down her cheeks. "I hate you," she sobs.

"I know."

She hugs me, but in the next moment, Cade is there. "I don't know what we're going to do with you," he sighs. His arms wrap around me and hold.

I close my eyes, fighting back the emotion of having come home again.

"Reid!" Mrs. Parker scolds. "You're supposed to be in bed."

I peek over Cade's shoulder to see his stumbling form make his way down the front steps. He looks crazed. My heart lodges in my throat as Cade moves out of the way in time for Reid to grab me. I stare into a pair of intoxicating green eyes. "Are you okay?" I ask, eyeing the raised lump in his hair line with a bandage over it.

Suddenly, all the oxygen gets taken away. I try to breathe in deep, but nothing comes. My eyes flare with panic, and my fingers sink into Reid's upper arms, trying to steady myself. My vision narrows. The world's falling away.

Something's wrong!, I scream inside. I can't bring in air.

Strong arms grip me from behind, hauling me into a chest. Lex skirts around Reid. "She's having a panic attack. Watch out." He brings me into the house and sets me down in the nice living room, the one they don't use. I'm sprawled across the designer sofa, staring up at the ceiling that feels like it's pressing down around me.

"Something's wrong. What's happening?" Reid curses. I try to focus on him, but the panic of feeling like I can't breathe takes over everything.

"Shh," Lex says, grabbing my hand. "You're having a panic attack. Just breathe. Relax."

Despite thinking I can't get any air, I take a breath and realize it's just an illusion. My lungs fill with oxygen. "I can't—"

Reid gets to his knees in front of me with a wince. The look on his face throws me into another bout. I clutch my chest as my heart feels like it explodes out of a racing gate.

"Should we call an ambulance?" Jules asks.

"She'll be okay," Lex and Mrs. Parker say at the same time. Lex continues with, "She just needs a moment."

Reid picks my hand off my chest and kisses my fingers. Instead of looking at his injury, I stare into his unwavering eyes. I can't believe I left this. I can't believe I left *him*.

I quickly change my thoughts because another feeling of helplessness starts to rise. Reid kisses my knuckles one by one, keeping his eyes on me. When his shoulders move up as he takes a breath, I follow suit, trying to even out.

"I'm sorry," I say immediately after the feeling passes. "I don't know what that was."

"That's your body reminding you that you need me," Reid says.

Mrs. Parker whispers something to Mr. Parker, and he disappears for a moment before returning with a glass of water. She squeezes in between Lex and Reid to hand it to me. "Sit up, Briar. Slowly. There you go." She puts a steady hand on my shoulders and offers me the glass. "I'm going to make something to eat. You look like you've lost weight." She stands, and Mr. Parker puts his arm around her shoulders as they move into the kitchen.

"Now I can't even be mad at you right now," Jules says. "Nice trick."

She grins, but I can tell she means it. Her eyes tell me we're going to have to discuss my leaving...at length. But there's guilt there, too.

Cade puts an arm around her shoulders. "I think she's in good hands for right now, why don't we give them some time?"

Jules nods. Lex and Reid part for her to give me a hug. Cade sneaks in to kiss me on the cheek, and they leave, the front door shutting behind them. When I look back, Reid has edged Lex out. He stands off to the side, his arms crossed as he watches.

I turn on my side, facing Reid. I know why I tried to shut all this out. If I remembered how good it felt to be so close to him, I would've come running back within the hour. "Are you okay?" I ask.

He grabs my hands again. "Are *you* okay? What did Sasha do?"

I shake my head. "Reid..." My throat thickens, threatening to keep everything inside again. "Your head. Are you okay?"

"I don't care about me," he grinds out.

"He's fine," Lex says, speaking up. "He got the laceration from the helmet. He had to get stitches, and he was out for a few hours. It's the concussion we're all worried about, but he's over the worst of it. He just needs to be monitored now."

An angry scowl makes its way across Reid's face. When Lex finishes giving me Reid's health update, Reid says, "Your turn. What happened? Are you okay?"

I shrug. "I'm fine." It's a lame answer, but I can't think of a better one at the moment.

"What were Sasha and Richards doing there?"

I close my eyes, feeling heat creep up my neck and spread over my cheeks.

Lex moves closer. "Richards had his shirt off. When I walked in, Briar was running toward the door, and Richards was holding his nuts."

A shadow falls over Reid. "Did he hurt you? Did he touch you?" With each question, his voice rises and the urgency behind his words promises he'll make this guy pay. All I have to do is say the words, and Reid would be out of this house in the next second, tracking that lowlife down. Concussion be damned.

I shake my head. I peek around Reid to make sure his parents are still in the kitchen and then say, "I guess

Sasha wanted more incriminating pictures of me. To show you. She thought if you saw that I ran away to be with someone else that you'd drop me. She started snapping pictures of that Richards guy standing in front of me with his fly down and his shirt off. When I tried to get away, he pinned me down on the bed. When she told him to move my shirt up, I panicked and kneed him in the balls."

"That's what she was doing with her phone, wasn't it?" Lex asks. When I nod, he sighs. "I should've fucking known." He looks down at Reid. "As soon as she heard the police were coming, she deleted the pictures. I thought she was trying to delete the other pic, so I told her not to bother. The police already saw it. I didn't know there were more."

"At least she doesn't have them anymore," I say. "Any of them."

"I'll kill him," Reid seethes. "I'll hunt that fucker down and chop off his nuts."

"We already owe him for that hit on you, brother," Lex says, like he's all down for that plan and then some.

Surrounded by the familiarity of these guys, I feel how tired I am. It's like I've let myself relax for the first time in a week. My defenses are down, and now all I want to do is rest. I didn't sleep well in the motel. Despite it's less than stellar cleaning record, my dreams woke me time and time again. "I missed you," I say, reaching out to touch Reid's face.

He holds my hand on his cheek, but the way he looks at me makes me think he's not entirely sure I'm telling the truth. I can't blame him. Why would he think I missed him if all I had to do was contact them to come back? "We have a lot to discuss," Reid says, his lips a tight line. He leans over and gives me a kiss on the cheek. I hold on to that moment, letting his kiss seal a promise to me. He doesn't like what I did. I knew he wouldn't. But maybe, just maybe, it doesn't change the way he feels about me.

"Her parents want her home soon. She called them on the way here. I didn't tell them we were stopping."

Reid scowls. "I don't want her out of my sight."

"Me either," Lex says. I tear my gaze away from Reid to find Lex staring at me with his big, brown eyes. "But that's not fair to them."

Reid's fingers grip me tighter like he can't bear to let me go. Behind him, his mom walks in to call us to the table. Lex shifts from foot to foot, casting a glance toward the door. After Reid helps me to my feet, I touch Lex's arm. "It's okay. We'll leave right after. My parents are going to be super pissed no matter what, so I might as well enjoy this last bit of freedom."

Mrs. Parker looks over her shoulder as she

approaches the table. "I'm sure your mother was just so worried, Briar."

I bite my lip. I'm sure she's worried, but the fact is, I made her worry again. I don't know how I can ever make that better.

4

If it's at all possible, I might even be more nervous to face my parents.

I know I screwed up. Last time I ran away, I didn't want to come back. I still had all the animosity for everything going on around me, but this time, I'm glad they found me. Maybe that's what I wanted the whole time, someone to rescue me. To catch me and shake me out of the hole I dug myself.

When Lex pulls into the driveway, he turns off the car, and we both just sit back. The front curtain moves, and my heart starts beating even faster. "You don't have to come in with me," I tell Lex. "This won't be pretty, and I deserve it."

He casts me a sideways glance. "I'm done standing back, Briar. I'm going in that house with you." He purses his lips. "I feel like I owe you an apology. I should've realized what you would do when you saw Reid hurt like that. It makes so much sense to me that you ran. Knowing I did nothing to help you when you were so...lost?" His throat moves like he's strangling himself from the inside out. "I fucked up."

"Hey," I say, grabbing his arm. "What I did was no one's fault but my own. I was stupid and acted carelessly." I shake my head. "I'm the one that should be apologizing to all of you. It was reckless and idiotic. It—."

"I don't want an apology," Lex says, speaking up. "I want your forgiveness."

His chestnut gaze locks onto mine, and my stomach overturns.

"In my eyes, I failed you. I don't care that you don't understand it. Just tell me you don't hate me. Tell me—"

I squeeze his arm. "Lex, I could never hate you."

His head falls back onto the seat with relief. His body visibly relaxes. The tension in the car is higher than ever though. My skin buzzes, and my neck itches. What I really need is a long, hot shower to wash the past week off me. And maybe an enema for my brain...

Lex throws his door open, so I follow. When we reach the front of the car, he grabs my hand and gives it a double pump that I barely notice because my eyes are on the front door. Right now, I can't think of a single reason why I wanted to leave this place. My parents. The house that holds almost all my favorite memories of Brady.

My heart constricts. Lex's hand in mine gives me the strength I need to twist the knob on the front door and push it open. Inside, my parents are sitting on the couch. They're both staring at their laps, and when we walk in, they glance up. My mom looks pale. My dad's hair is disheveled. I stare at them even though it pains me to do so because I know I did that to them.

I wiggle free of Lex's hand and cross the floor, dropping to my knees in front of them. Shame. Humiliation. Self-loathing. All of it hits me at that moment. My eyes burn and run over with salty tears. "I'm sorry." I hug them both, my hands encapsulating their upper legs, my left around my mother and my right around my father like I can show them with gestures that I didn't mean to leave. I truly didn't. It just felt right at the time.

A hand comes down on my head. I feel a pat, pat, and I know right away it's my father. "You scared us again, Briar."

"I know," I say, choking back a sob. "I won't do it again."

"That's what you said last time," my mother says, her voice curt.

I don't actually remember saying that last time, but I might have to get them to forgive me.

My mother's stiff. I peer up at her, my eyelashes spiked in front of me. When she looks at me, her face softens. "Why, Briar? Just why?"

I clutch at my chest again. My heart starts racing and despair hits me, making me feel as if I'm hurtling toward a brick wall.

Lex kneels next to me. His arm goes around my shoulders. "Shh. It's okay. Deep breaths."

My eyes go out of focus, but I think I see my mother staring at him like a stranger.

"I think she's having major anxiety or even panic attacks. She had one on the way home."

Even though I'm concentrating on my breathing, I don't miss the lie of omission he just spouted for me. Technically, I had one at Reid's house, but we're not telling my parents about the stop we made.

I wrap my hand in his and squeeze. After a few moments, my breathing returns to normal, and I feel as if I can think clearly again. Mom and Dad are still staring at me, so I steel my shoulders. "Something happened when Reid was in the hospital. I started to crack. I don't know. It reminded me so much of Brady, and then I just started to itch all over. I wanted to leave. I wanted to get away from it all because it hurt too much."

"That's understandable," Dad says.

Mom casts him a furious look. "It's understandable that you would feel that way, Briar, but when you get like that, you need to tell someone. Running away is not the answer."

"I know," I tell her.

Her gaze narrows a fraction, like she's trying to figure out if I'm just saying what she wants to hear to get out of punishment, but I'm not.

Lex rubs my back. His massive hands sink a steady pressure into me. I close my eyes and breathe. "I really am so sorry."

Mom stands, making me move back. "I'm glad you're okay, Briar, but I think time will tell whether you're actually sorry or not." She starts to walk away, but turns around. "I'd get some sleep if I were you, you're going to school tomorrow."

Dad stands afterward, bringing me to my feet. He kisses me on the cheek. "We love you, Briar."

"I love you too."

He follows Mom, leaving Lex and I in the living room. It feel so empty in here without them. "What do you need me to do?" Lex asks.

I shrug. "Nothing. I'm just going to take a shower and go to bed." I turn toward him. "Thank you for being here though."

He stares at the carpet. I know he doesn't want to leave, but I'm not in danger of running away again tonight—most likely ever.

I stand on my tiptoes to hug him. His hands come around my back, squeezing me to him. "Don't worry about me, Lex. I promise I'll be fine."

"It's impossible for me not to worry about you."

I start to pull away, and Lex's phone rings. He looks down at the screen and answers. By his next words, I know it's Reid on the other end of the line. "Yeah, I just dropped her off."

He lifts his gaze to meet mine, and his lips turn into a thin line. I walk toward the front door, so he has no choice but to follow me. I open it for him. He gives me one last weary look and steps outside. "Bye," I mouth.

He just stares, his phone to his ear while he listens to whatever Reid's saying, so I wave and close the door, leaving his heavy gaze on the other side.

I pad to the bathroom, turning on the light when I walk in. It's the same as I left it. I don't even think my parents came in here when I was gone. I strip the clothes I've been wearing for a week and cleaning in the motel room sink off before stepping into the shower. I turn the shower spray on, letting it run from lukewarm to hotter than Hades, hoping it will scald some of my skin away. I shampoo my hair, remembering how Reid did that for me once in this very same tub. My stomach bottoms out, and I clutch the side of the tub. Once the water's run clear, I turn off the faucet and squeeze the water out of my hair.

I move the shower curtain aside and stare right into the big, square bathroom mirror. My hair's fully back to its original color now. My skin is pale like my mother's, and my eyelashes are still wet like they were when I was crying. I grab a towel on the rack and wrap myself with it before moving to my room at the end of the hall. My bed is made, which I'm pretty sure I didn't do before I left that day, and my phone is sitting on the edge. My old phone, the one I tossed when I was near the hospital. Somehow, someone had gotten it back. I thought for sure it would've been stolen right away, even if I did toss it into a line of bushes.

I grab it and hit the screen. Miraculously, it brightens to life in my hands. When I check the battery level, I realize someone has already charged it for me. There are hundreds of texts and missed calls.

CALL ME.

WHY ARE YOU DOING THIS?

BRIAR, WE'RE WORRIED.

YOU LEFT ME?
I MEAN IT, CALL ME.
WHERE ARE YOU?
I LOVE YOU.

My breath hitches. I stare down at the screen, reading and rereading that text. While I stand, there's a knock on my bedroom window. When I look up, I see Reid. His palm is pressed against the glass. I toss my phone on the bed and move that way. I take the screen out and lift the window. "What are you doing?" I hiss. "I thought you had to take it easy."

He waits until he's in my room, staring at me. "My girlfriend comes home, and you don't think I'm going to be by her side whenever I can?"

"You have a concussion. It's serious."

"So is loving you."

I take a step back, but he holds me in place. His eyes get a faraway look. "I feel like maybe I heard you say this. It's a vague memory, almost like a dream. But when I was in the hospital, did you tell me you loved me?"

My chin wobbles. I bite my lip to try to stop it, but it doesn't work, so I end up nodding.

"I tried to say it back, but I don't think the words came out. In my head, I was screaming them. I was telling you how much I loved you. I knew the look in your eyes, but there wasn't anything I could fucking do about it, so let me say this one thing. I fucking love you, Briar. You don't ever have to run away from me or anything else ever again because as long as I have control, I swear I won't let anything bad happen. I might've been trapped in my head, but I was fighting. I was fighting for us. I was fighting for you. I'll always fight."

I move to my tiptoes and press my lips to his. I leave them there, savoring the moment like he's the perfect day and I can't get enough of it. Eventually, he deepens the kiss, forcing my mouth open so he can delve inside. He moves me back until my knees hit the bed, and then he's slowly lowering me to the mattress.

Fire heats my core as he presses into me. He's already hard, ready, and waiting. His hand moves to my chest, unravels my towel and opens both sides, taking his time getting his fill of me. "You're so unbelievably beautiful."

He dips his head to kiss a line down my chest, between my breasts to my belly button and back up. My knees drift open, and he nuzzles himself between my legs, grinding against me.

I don't know how or why I left this, this safe space. I can't exactly explain it, but I know it had something to do with the fear of never feeling any of this again.

Of never having Reid look at me the way he is right now. Of never having him touch me like this again. I didn't run away from him. I ran away because I didn't want to face a world where he was gone too. I thought I could just shut it out. I thought if I didn't know, it would be better. I can't face a world without Brady *and* Reid.

"I wanted to be there for you," I say in between kisses. "I was scared. I thought I was going to lose you."

His hot mouth lowers to my nipple. My head drops back as he pulls it into his mouth with a gentle suck. Heat makes a war cry toward my core until I need him there. I pull his shirt up until he has to move back to help me take it off. It ends up on the floor and then I start with his jeans. I work the button through the hole and slide my hands inside, grabbing him until he moans. "Christ, Briar."

I work him in tune with his subtle grinding until we're both clawing at his clothes to get them off. Before his jeans drop, he grabs his wallet and takes out a condom, throwing it next to us on the bed.

He crawls back over me. "I missed you in every way possible. Not just this, but your quiet strength. Just being next to you eases my soul. I didn't even realize it until you weren't there."

"I should never have left you like that," I tell him,

pressing my hands to his cheeks. "I'll never forgive myself."

He drops his forehead to mine. His body shakes like a current, and he's sweeping me right along with it. He closes his eyes, taking a deep breath before reaching for the condom, ripping the package open, and taking it out. He rolls it over him while I stare into his face, seeing it for the first time in what feels like forever. When he looks back at me, he poises himself at my entrance. He bites his lip and pushes inside. I gasp, sighing when he's fully seated.

He lets out a breath, dropping his head to my chest. "Fuck me." A shiver courses over his body as he starts to move. First, with all the precaution someone should have with a concussion, but then faster like he can't get enough. I hold on to him, reveling in the way we come together until he's revved me all the way up and then some.

My toes start to curl as the feeling unfurls. "Reid," I gasp out.

His attentions quicken, driving his need higher along with my own until I come. I press my lips together to keep from screaming and dig my fingernails into his arms. His body jerks inside me. He grunts, the noise loud in the otherwise quiet room.

Moving inside me until he shudders, he drapes

himself over me after kissing my nose. "I'm staying with you tonight," he breathes. "I already told my parents. I'll leave a little early, then come back and get you before school."

I nod into him, wrapping my body around him while we fall to our sides. There, I find the safest, coziest place I can and fall asleep in Reid's arms.

5

As promised, Reid leaves early. He doesn't slip out unnoticed. He wakes me up, kissing me, telling me he loves me and that he'll see me in a little while. He goes out the same way he came in, and I snuggle under my blankets as he lowers the window. I'll have to put the screen back when I get up, but I just watch the window for a moment, even when he's left and I've heard a car start up down the street.

After a few minutes, I pull myself out of bed, fix the screen, and head into the shower. The guys, thankfully, saved me from everyone at school looking at me again with the story they told. Everyone knew I'd run away before. Now, everyone thinks I was at my grandparents' house if they thought about me at all.

I take a shower, dress in something appropriate, dry my hair, and put makeup on. For the first time in a while, I put all my energy into getting ready for school. When I first opened the closet, I noticed my bookbag was there, too, probably retrieved from Jules's car at some point over the last week. Pulling it up my shoulder, I walk from my room and into the dining room. No one's up yet when I get there. I'm still a little tired from everything that happened recently, but honestly, I did a whole lot of nothing while I was at the motel other than the time it took to scrounge up the one night's motel fee and some money for a bit of food. Checking the time, I realize I'm early and decide to make breakfast. I pull out the eggs, the griddle, and a loaf of bread and start making French toast. By the time my mom comes down the hall from the opposite side of the house, I already have the first four slices ready.

She pauses in the entryway, blinking at me.

"Good morning," I say, my cheeks reddening.

She unties and reties her robe. "You're making breakfast?"

I shrug because it's obvious what I'm doing. I think my mom is just searching for something to say.

My dad comes out next, dressed in a pair of suit pants and a nice polo. He stops just behind Mom, smiling. "Breakfast? Awesome."

He angles around her and sits at the bar. I pull out a serving platter and dish up the French toast that's done already. My mom still stands in the entryway while my father takes two slices, pouring syrup over them like nothing's bothering him.

"Are they okay?" I ask after he takes his first bite.

He smiles. "Delicious, honey."

The doorbell rings. I've just put the next batch on the griddle, so I skip off to answer it, knowing it's Reid. I give him a huge smile when I open the door. He's leaning against the pillar, his hands shoved in his pockets. For a moment, I realize how normal this all is. In another life, before Brady, before I decided to run away, I could see this very same thing happening. Now that everything's changed, it's still happening. It hits me then: Life really does move on no matter what. Your world could turn upside down in one moment, but the Earth keeps rotating. Other people carry on. Even you, on the outside, still keep up a face. But right here, right now? This actually does feel normal, not out-of-place.

"Hey," I say, a little breathless just seeing him there waiting for me like that.

He smirks. "Hey."

He moves forward, placing his hands on my hips, and then leans over to give me a peck on the mouth.

My cheeks go up in flames. "Remember my parents don't know yet," I whisper.

"I know," he says, lifting his hands. "I'll keep my hands to myself. For now."

He walks around me and into the house. After shutting the door, I hurry after him.

"Hello, Reid."

"Good morning," he says happily.

"How's your head?"

My shoulders deflate. I'd been so busy staring at how hot he looked, I forgot to check the lump on his head and the stitches. They should really stick out to me, but they don't. I just see him. "Been better," he says. "Still got the worst of all headaches, but the doctor said that shouldn't last too much longer."

My dad smiles as I return to the griddle to flip the French toast. When I turn, Reid is eyeing me. I know he, too, wants to say something about me making breakfast, but instead, he sits. When the next four are finished, I give him two and save two for myself while I make some more.

When Reid came in, Mom ventured to the bar. She's slowly eating her French toast. She hasn't let her guard down yet, and I can't blame her. I wouldn't be able to either. While Reid and Dad talk football, I ask, "Are you going to work today, Mom?"

She blinks then glances up at me. "Your dad's going in this morning. I haven't been going, but I think I'll make it in this afternoon now that everything is... better here."

I don't know how to talk to this mom. I can talk to the mom who loves me, and I can even talk to the mom who is yelling at me, but the one who seems so out of sorts she doesn't know what's going on? I'm not sure I know how to deal with that. Instead of saying anything back, I give her a small smile and stuff my face with the rest of my last mouthful. I flip the last four slices and serve them up on the platter as Reid stands from his chair. "We should probably go, Briar."

This gets Mom's attention. "You don't have to take her, Reid. I can take her."

He looks at her robe and lifts an eyebrow. This makes my mom take a look too. She turns red from her neck all the way to her hairline. "It's absolutely fine. I want to take her."

Mom ties and reties her robe, then nods in submission. I pull my bookbag up my shoulder. "I'll see you guys later."

Out of the corner of my eye, I see my mom prod my dad, hitting him in the upper arm and then nodding toward me. "Oh, honey," he says. "With everything that's going on, your mom and I would like you back home right after school."

I turn toward them. "I understand."

"That means you're grounded," Mom says, her tone harsh.

"I understand," I say again. I expected this.

Behind me, Reid opens the front door, so I turn on my heel and leave. He waits for me just outside, throwing his arms around me when I step out. "Breakfast, huh? Buttering them up?"

I shake my head. "It wasn't about that. I was the first one up, so I thought I should do something."

He leans over and kisses my temple. I hope my mom isn't watching from the window because I need to be the one to tell them about Reid and me. Maybe tonight when I get home from school. Reid opens the car door for me and steps back. "Your mom took this time pretty rough. She thought you were past all the running away shit, so it blindsided her again."

Guilt slides over me. "I thought I was over it too," I whisper.

Reid puts a finger under my chin, making me look him in the eyes. "She'll come around, babe." He glances over his shoulder back toward the house. "Do you have any idea how hard it is not to kiss you right now? Or sneak back in through your bedroom and screw school all together?"

A smile filters over my face. "I do know, actually."

He shrugs. "I guess we can't have it all."

He shuts my door, walks around to the other side, and gets in. "Hey, how did you get out of the house again?" I prod. Lex made it seem as if his mom had him on lockdown.

"I told my mom you were going to school today, and that I wasn't going to let you out of my sight. I swear she's only agreeing to any of this because it's you. If it was anyone else, she'd probably have me chained to the bed. She really likes the idea of you and me together."

I hope my parents feel the same way. "But what about the doctors, Reid? Are you well enough to go back to school?"

"I've been feeling fine, really. Just a headache. Sometimes I can't concentrate, but there's nothing physically limiting me from going back. Plus, the quicker I get back to school, the quicker I can go to practice and show Coach I'm ready to play."

I stare straight ahead as he pulls out of the driveway and points the car toward school. I hadn't thought about Reid going back to football. I tried not to think about him, but when I did, I pictured him injured. Laid up with broken bones. I was not prepared for him to say he was going back to playing so soon. "Do you think that's a good idea?"

Reid keeps one hand on the steering wheel and places the other on my thigh. He sends me a cautious look. "It's...yes. Briar, I'm going back to football. I love it. Not going back isn't an option, plus, you know college scouts are out already. That's my ticket out of here."

He sounds just like Brady. I know how much football means to all four of them, but haven't there been enough injuries now? What if he gets hurt again? What if Cade or Lex get hurt? Or worse?

Panic claws at my chest. Preemptively, I slow my breathing, counting to five as I inhale and exhale to keep it under control.

"I know it's hard," Reid says, "But just remember what I said. If it's in my control, nothing's happening to either one of us. I'll be extra careful. Lex already feels like shit, so he's going to be watching like a hawk. Trust me, when I get back out onto that field, I'll be one-hundred percent. You won't have to worry at all."

His words soothe me a little. Maybe just a fraction. I'll still always worry, but I know I can't let that interfere either. "So, they're playing Barnhardt now?" I ask, referring to the backup QB.

Reid takes a left and then returns his hand back to me. "Yeah. Coach has to. I'll be back at practice, so hopefully I can help him until I can get back out there." Reid makes a face, and I remember a time when Brady had lamented Spring Hill's backup QB. There's a clear reason why he's the backup and why Reid's the starter. Barnhardt probably never thought he'd get the chance to play. Reid's the real deal. I wouldn't be surprised if he gets multiple offers from different colleges. He's been All-State every year since we were Freshman, along with Brady, Lex, and Cade.

I place my hand on top of his. "I'm sure he'll do his best and that you'll be good at coaching him until you're ready."

Reid doesn't answer because the school looms in front of us. Thanks to the guys, I don't have as much nerves as I did when I first came back at the beginning of the year. "Lex got your homework for you. I'm sure he has it on him."

As if on cue, there's a knock on my window. I jump, my hand going over my chest. Relief floods me when I realize it's just Lex, and I smile. He pulls the car door open. "Sorry, Briar. I didn't mean to."

"It's not your fault," I tell him. "Just jumpy I guess."

Like Reid thought, Lex offers me my homework. He has it organized by class in a singular folder. Behind him, I see Theo Laughlin walk by and wonder if I still have any shot of beating him. I turn toward Reid as he gets out of the car. I only see his profile before it disappears above the frame of the car, but that's enough. He told me he loved me. I can't imagine not going to the same school he's going to. Or to the same school as all of them for that matter. They're my group, my tribe, my *friends*.

An arm drops around my shoulder from behind and a kiss drops to the top of my head. "Shortie, look at you."

I smile up at Cade. His dark hair is longer than it was only a week ago. It's past the time where he usually gets it cut. It almost looks unkempt, giving Cade even more of that bad boy look that girls love.

"Tell me you're going to practice tonight," Cade says, looking over at Reid. He lowers his voice. "I think Barnhardt's going to shit himself."

All three of the guys laugh. Quick footsteps come up behind me, and I turn in time to see Jules making her way over. A lot of the worried texts were hers, so I open my arms and hug her like I should've done yesterday. "I promise we'll talk," I say, whispering in her ear.

She softens at my touch, hugging me back. "We better."

When I pull away, I say, "I'm grounded though. I have to be home right after school."

"I'll take you," she says. "Maybe we can talk then?"

I nod. Now, my stomach twists in anticipation. I know she might not have the nicest things to say to me right now, and she'd be right. I have to listen to it. I have to take it all in and figure out how I'm going to make it up to her.

Turning back toward the school, my eyes drift from the top of the flags waving in the wind right down to the front doors. All five of us move forward as a group. It isn't until we're halfway to the glass doors that I realize that walking into school together was probably all planned. They wanted to be here for me.

Or, it's because they don't trust me to be where I say I'm going to be. Either way, I'm glad they're here.

"Hey, isn't that…?"

Cade stops. He hits Reid in the chest, and then like a domino effect, each of us stop to stare as Sasha gets out of a Lincoln SUV near the front of the school. My blood curdles at the sight of her, but that's not who has all our attention though. It's the dark-haired boy walking next to her.

"You're shitting me," Reid says.

Lex growls. "What the fuck?"

Jules and I exchange a look. We don't know who this guy is, but we know something's just happened. And it's not good.

6

We follow the pair into the school. Reid's steps are hurried, so I have to walk double to keep up with him. Sasha and the mystery boy stop in the football hangout area near the stairs, right by where Reid's locker is. Sasha hugs her cheerleader girlfriends while her new friend looks around. Apparently, sometime in the week I've been gone, Sasha dumped her lacrosse boyfriend. It's weird she had time to do that considering she was having fun making my life miserable.

Bitch.

A few of the football players eye the guy warily. I can tell they know who he is, too. It feels like Jules and I are the only ones who don't. When they see Reid, though, they break out into smiles. "Parker. Fuck, man," a guy on the offensive line says. He comes over and claps him on the back. "Good to see you, dude."

When the guy lets him go, Reid grabs my hand again, his fingers tight on my own. He side-eyes the newcomer, but answers the guy. "Good to be back, man."

The other football guys gather around Reid. They all ask how he's doing and express the fact they're thrilled he's back. A few of them even lower their voices to tell him Barnhardt needs some serious help.

"That's what I've been told," Reid responds with a grin.

"Poor fucker never thought he'd get a chance."

Sasha saunters into the middle of the group, pushing past two huge guys like they're nothing. This is so cliché high school, I think, as she moves in. Of course, the cheerleaders and the football team hang out in the exact same area of the school. She puts a hand on her hip, and I squeeze Reid's hand right back. When she first came into the motel room, I have to admit, I was afraid. But not right now. Not with these guys surrounding me. "Did you have fun last night?" I ask.

Her eyes flash for a second, but no one knows what happened yesterday but us, so she's not going to take my bait. She doesn't want the whole school to know she got in trouble for having underage sexual pictures on her phone. What I'd really like to know, though, is why she seems so damn happy? She must've only gotten a slap on the wrist at best. The Pontine's do it again, sweeping everything under the rug.

She beams in the next second, then places her dainty hand on her hip. "I did, actually," she says, smiling what seems like a genuine smile until you see the hardness in her eyes. She reaches her hand out. "You guys know Oscar, right?"

All gazes shift toward him. I can tell he's fine with the attention. He beams. His tanned skin and dark eyes dance under the fluorescent lights. His dark hair is gelled, parted to the side with the sides shaved. "What's up, fellas?"

Reid stiffens. I wish I knew what was going on. I'm completely in the dark. I only know Reid and the guys are practically fuming underneath the surface. Oscar moves forward, hand outstretched to Reid. Reid ignores him, not even bothering his offer of civility a spare glance.

"My dad gave Oscar's mom a job in town, so they moved here a couple of days ago."

Oscar hikes his bookbag up his shoulder as if he's showing it off.

"Wait. You go here now?" Reid asks.

Oscar nods. "My mom couldn't turn down the generous offer by the Pontine's."

Cade is the first one of our group to speak up. "In the middle of the season? Why the hell would you do that? You had a good thing going at Rawley Heights."

Oscar shrugs noncommittally. "You know. Family shit."

Sasha places her arm around him, cementing herself to his side. If any of the other girls were charmed by Oscar's good looks, she just claimed him in front of the entire school. "My dad just had to have Oscar's mom."

"I bet he did," one of the players says under his breath.

"Not like that," Sasha spits. She tries to regain composure, but I can tell the comment affected her. When I glance at Oscar though, his face is red with anger. He definitely didn't like that comment.

"Come on," Reid says, pulling back on my hand to steer me away. The halls are filled now with the steady hum of morning excitement before classes kick in.

"Who's this?" Oscar asks, catching everyone's attention. Reid comes to a stop, and I nearly bump into him. "I remember you two being together," Oscar says, looking back and forth between Sasha and Reid.

"I dumped him," Sasha says, sneering.

Everyone in this damn group knows that's a lie. They were all there for the very public argument between the two of them at the homecoming party.

Reid puts his arm around my shoulders. "My girlfriend Briar."

Oscar looks me up and down, making me feel like I'm under a microscope.

"Brady's sister," Sasha whispers, like what Reid and I are doing is risqué.

Oscar's eyebrows pop. "No shit. It's nice to meet you, Briar. Brady was—."

I don't hear the rest of what the new kid, Oscar, has to say because Reid steers me away again. Lex and Cade follow behind us, and soon, Jules is at my side. "That's Oscar Diego, isn't it?" she asks.

Now I know I'm the only one who has no idea what's going on.

"Yep," Lex says, his voice filled with unrestrained menace.

"Reid..." Jules says, trailing off as if there's a lot to say, but she doesn't have the words to express what's going on.

"I know," he grits out.

"Does someone want to clue me in as to what's going on?"

We get to my locker and form our own little group.

Lex peers back down the hallway and then turns toward us, his gaze finally settling on me. "Oscar Diego is the quarterback for Rawley Heights football team."

"Seven's backup on the All-State team," Cade adds.

I blink up at Reid as realization dawns on me. Sasha just brought Reid's competition to our school. And with perfect timing, too, since he's injured and can't play. "That fucking bitch," I growl.

"She did this on purpose," Jules says, tossing a look over her shoulder toward the other group. "She may have even planned it from the beginning."

Reid bends down, kissing the top of my head. He does it so hard it kind of startles me, but then he walks away, going in the opposite direction of where he used to rule over the group. "Stay with Briar," he demands before turning down the next hallway and disappearing from sight.

Cade leans against the locker next to mine, his head coming back to rest against the steel. "This is not fucking good."

"Coach won't play Oscar though," I say.

"Why wouldn't he?" Lex asks.

"Well, first, we're in the middle of the damn season."

"We don't have a good quarterback right now," Cade says, shaking his head. "Barnhardt is fucking worthless. Coach Jackson is going to jump at this."

"But he can't replace Reid," I say. The thought doesn't even register with me. Why in the hell would he do that? Reid's been so good to him. "Besides, we don't even know if Oscar's going to play football."

Lex and Cade blink at me. Jules steps forward. "He's good, Briar. I remember Brady talking about him giving Reid a run for his money."

"But Reid's still the best," I counter.

"Not right now, he isn't," Cade says, kicking off the wall. "I'm going to see what I can find out."

Lex moves in close to Jules and me. The warning bell rings overhead. Jules leaves, shaking her head, while I open my locker to retrieve everything I need for the first part of the day.

"I can't believe I let that fucker get in on him."

"It wasn't your fault," I say, stuffing the last notebook into my bag before shutting the locker door and spinning the lock.

Lex puts his hand on the small of my back, leading me to homeroom. "It *was* my fault," he says, his voice barely audible through the scramble to get to first period.

As soon as I step inside, his hand leaves, and when I look behind me, he's gone.

I stare at the empty space. *Maybe I should take this more seriously than I originally thought.*

7

Classes feel like a foreign prison. That's the thing with taking time off with absolutely nothing to do and no one to talk to. Real life feels so structured and restrictive. What I really want to do is find Reid and pick his brain about this Oscar kid, but I don't have any classes with him. At best, all I can hope for is to talk to him during lunch.

That is, until English class rolls around. I take my seat in the back and stare straight ahead. My foot jumps up and down. I now only have about an hour until I can see the guys and Jules again to figure out what is going on because obviously I'm missing something. I peek at the clock again when a dark-haired guy saunters into the room. My gaze tracks over to him, and my body immediately locks. Oscar's in this class. Shit.

I shift uncomfortably. The only empty seat in the whole class is right next to me, and I silently curse the fact that I'm rebelling against my former self and sitting in the back of the class when I usually sit in the front.

The girls in the room immediately latch onto him. They watch him with their eyes. He is good looking. I can see why Sasha's all over him. She likes new and shiny, but in the same respect, she likes the traditional, too. That's why she'd still take Reid if she could.

"Hey," Oscar says. I'm explicitly trying not to look at him, which means I'm pretty much the only one in the class who isn't. "Yoohoo," he says. "Briar, right?"

I turn as he sits in the empty seat. He nods, acknowledging me, but I turn back toward the front. Whoever this guy is, if he's friends with Sasha, he isn't a friend of mine.

I'm dying to know what happened between Sasha and the police. I could probably ask, considering I'm the one who's in the picture she had on her phone, but the police also don't know it was me. Even though she's here acting like nothing happened, that can't possibly be true, right? They had to do something to her, didn't they? It's not like she could've just gotten off with a slap on the wrist and a stern talking to.

Around me, the grinding of chairs against the

decade old tile in the room erupts. I focus in to see people pairing up. I look around frantically, until Mr. Shaver says, "Oscar, Briar, you're partners since neither of you were here when the assignment was announced." He walks toward us, handing each of us a piece of paper with the heading Literary Assignment. I scan the room and find Theo partnered with another girl who's in the top ten of the class. Of course, he is. Damn.

"Mr. Shaver, I'd like to work by myself," I say before he can turn away.

The mid-life crisis teacher—he got an earring last year—looks up. "No can do. Part of this is learning how to work with other people. Besides, don't we want to welcome the new kid to the school?"

He turns around without waiting for my answer. As I glare at his back, I realize pretty much every girl in the class is giving me a dirty look. I close my eyes and try to count to ten while I hear a snicker to the side of me. "You don't like me, do you?"

"I don't know you."

"Exactly," he says.

"But I do know Sasha," I say, finally turning toward him. "She's not my friend."

Oscar lifts his shoulders. "Is this a catty girl thing?

You're dating her ex-boyfriend, so you automatically have to hate each other?"

"No, it's a she's a fucking cunt thing."

His eyes round. "Huh. I had you pegged differently, but I like it."

His cocky smirk ticks me off. It's like he's placating me, and whatever that look in his eyes is, I feel like he knows a lot more about what's going on than he's letting show. "So, you and her?"

"Friends."

I give him a doubtful look.

"No one said friends without benefits. We're not wearing promise rings or anything if that's what you're asking."

I suddenly regret I asked. I peer down at the paper, quickly skimming through everything and realize we have to do a report together on a classic body of work or a classic writer. For the rest of the period, we talk over who we'd like to do it on and then check with Mr. Shaver as we leave to make sure no one else picked it already. I was really hoping for Jane Austen, but we settled on The Great Gatsby.

Since we're the last two out of class, we inevitably walk side by side down the hall. It only takes me a moment to realize he's going to lunch too, which means he'll probably be sitting at our table. Or what used to be our table.

"Briar," a voice calls out. I stop. Footsteps rush toward us from behind and then a strong arm lands around my shoulders. I look up to find Lex staring at Oscar with narrowed eyes.

Oscar looks at the two of us, mostly how close we are with his arm wrapped around my shoulders. He makes a face that looks like he's filing away this information for later. The back of my neck burns, and an instinct kicks in to move as far away from Lex as possible. It's not that I mind when he puts his arm around me like this, it's just that I think Oscar is getting the wrong idea. He doesn't understand how close we all are.

"Lex," Oscar says, nodding at him.

He walks ahead of us. Lex leans down. "What's going on?"

I shrug. "Just walking to lunch."

When we enter the cafeteria, my gaze moves across the array of tables to see if we're still sitting in the same place. There's a crowd around our table. It isn't until someone leaves that I notice it's a crowd around Reid. He looks up, finding Lex and I walking through the entryway and stands.

I walk toward him, brushing past Oscar in the

process. Reid isn't looking at me anymore though. His attention is behind me, most likely on Lex. It isn't until I'm right next to him that he finally looks at me, forcing a smile to his face. "There's my girl."

"Hey," I say, worry working its way into my voice. "Are you okay?"

Reid shrugs, but motions toward the table. The crowd around him disperses as we sit. "I got your lunch."

"What about you?"

"I'm not hungry."

"Oscar!" a voice calls out.

I look behind Reid to see that the cheerleaders have taken over the table next to ours. They're all waving for him to sit with them. He does so with a cocky grin on his face.

Reid pulls me to his side, kissing the top of my head as Lex sits across from us. Jules comes along a couple of minutes later with a tray of food and sits.

I want to ask Cade what he found out, but oddly enough, he's not here. Instead, I ask Reid, "What's going on?"

"Nothing," Reid answers. "Eat up. My mom was right. You lost some weight while you were at your grandparents' house."

I exchange a look with Jules and start to eat what's

on my tray. When I came back and realized Reid hadn't been as badly hurt as I had imagined, I thought things would go back to normal. Sure, Sasha would be there, and she'd be a bitch, but I didn't expect this. I feel like there's a cloud of questions hovering over us. Reid shifts uneasily next to me, and even Lex keeps throwing glances toward the cheerleading table. They really don't like that he's here. Is it just because he seems to be friends with Sasha or is it the football thing?

Lunch is one of the oddest I've had here. Barely any of us talk. I know there's a lot unsaid between all of us because I ran away again, but it seems like more than that too.

One of the guys on the basketball team walks by and snickers when he sees me. Reid's off in his own little world, so he doesn't see when the guy pointedly drops his gaze to my chest and sneers.

My face blooms red. Lex notices and looks up to find the guy walking away.

My breath leaves my chest. He must've seen the picture. A quick check behind me, and I see him heading to sit with the cheerleaders. It makes sense. She might not have blasted it all over the school like she'd planned, but she definitely showed some people.

"You okay?" Lex asks.

This makes Reid look up.

"I'm—"

"Christ. Lex. Back the fuck up," Reid growls low under his breath. His arm moves around me possessively.

Lex cocks his head, moving his gaze to his friend. "There's something clearly wrong."

Reid stiffens. "There is, actually. And it's not Briar."

Lex and Reid hold each other's gaze for so long that it makes me want to crawl under the table. Eventually, Lex stands. He looks from me to Reid and then walks away.

"What's going on?"

"Don't worry about it," Reid says.

"I am worrying about it," I tell him, turning into his chest. "Are you guys fighting or something?"

He stares into my eyes and then looks away, cursing under his breath. He stands. "I'll see you after school." He walks a couple steps away, then turns back, leaning down to kiss me on the lips.

He heads the same way Lex left. Jules and I both watch after them. Once Reid leaves, I look over at Jules. "Are they fighting?"

Jules blows out a breath. "It's Lex, Briar. He loves you."

I blink. "What?"

"He loves you," she says. "It's written all over his face. Seeing you guys together probably tears him up inside."

My stomach churns with guilt. "Reid said he talked to him."

"That's not going to make it go away. I was watching them yesterday at Reid's house. They both acted like you were theirs. That shit isn't going to fly with Reid," she says, lowering her voice. "And I know he was angry he couldn't go to the hotel to get you himself. He wanted to be the one who did it. I've never seen him so angry."

The bell rings overhead, and Jules and I both take our trays to the tray return and dump them inside. I bite my lip, thinking about the way Reid looked at Lex and I when we walked in. Oscar had looked at us funny too. "Should I talk to him? To Lex?"

Jules shrugs. "I don't know that you can do anything," she says. "It's just going to suck for a while. You know, seeing someone you love be with someone else."

My mind keeps catching on the L word. Does Lex really *love* me? Like that? I know he had feelings for me. Maybe still has feelings for me, but love?

"Move it, flat chest." A shoulder collides with mine, and I stumble out of the way.

I look up to see a cheerleader throw me a taunting grin over her shoulder.

"Back off, bitch," Jules growls out.

The girl doesn't stop. She just laughs, sauntering down the hall. We stare after her, my mind trying not to focus on what she said. On what that really means.

How many people have seen the picture of me? Just how many fucking people did Sasha show it to?

"Forget them," Jules says quickly.

"She showed it to people," I say automatically.

Jules takes my shirt and drags me toward my locker. "Who cares? At best, all they have is her word that it was you. Just act like you have no idea what they're talking about."

"That doesn't take away the fact that they've seen my...my boob, Jules. Shit." I sigh and turn toward my locker, cutting in front of two Freshman to replace my books. When I get there, though, I stop in my tracks. There's a paper taped to the top. It has two tiny circles with two little dots inside them along with the words.

#7 likes tiny titties.

A hand comes from behind me and grabs it. I almost shriek, but a warm hand on my back and Reid's growl in my ear alerts me to who's actually there. "Who did this?"

"I don't know."

A smooth voice comes from behind. "Aww." We both turn to see Oscar, Sasha pressed against his side. He isn't holding her protectively, not like Reid is with me. She has her hand on his chest, like she's more of an adornment for him, which he doesn't seem to mind at all. "Like that matters," he says. "All you need is a handful."

Sasha sneers. "That's not what you said last night." She blatantly sticks out her chest, catching his attention. He ogles her, taking his time, before he looks back up.

He winks at me and then shrugs. "See you at practice, Reid."

They start to walk away. My breath hitches in my throat. He'll see him at practice? No, this isn't happening. Sasha turns around, blowing Reid a kiss before facing forward again and sliding her hand into Oscar's back pocket.

That used to be them. Reid and Sasha. Now it's Sasha and Oscar, and Reid has been delegated to the guy who likes tiny titties.

When I look up, Reid's frozen. He's staring after

the two of them, a murderous look on his face. "Reid?" I say, trying to get his attention back, but he pulls away.

"I have to go to practice tonight," he says stiffly. "Get Jules to take you home."

"Reid?" I say, my voice tinged with a hint more desperation. He turns, crumbling the paper in his fist and throwing it into the nearest trash can as he walks away.

8

Throughout the rest of the day, several more people make pointed comments about my chest. I never really had a complex about that one area of my body, but shame hits me hard the more people bring it up. I'm embarrassed about the picture itself. I'm embarrassed about the realities behind that picture. I sent it to Sasha for crying out loud. I'm almost surprised she kept it this long without showing everybody. It shows how truly diabolical she is.

Jules waits for me by my locker. I load up my bookbag with every textbook I have. I have so much to catch up on. Thanks to Lex, though, I have all the assignments I need to make up while I was "at my grandparents' house".

All the way home, I think about all the work I have

to do, and before I know it, Jules is pulling into my driveway. My father's car is in the garage with the garage bay door open. I reach over to open the door, but a word from Jules stops me. "Seriously?"

I look over at her. She glances away, shaking her head.

A muscle in my stomach tightens. "I'm sorry, Jules. I'm out of it. Do you want to come in so we can talk?"

"No," she says. "I want to talk right here, and I just want to talk while you listen."

Her lower lip quivers, but she steels her shoulders and turns angry eyes on me. I'm so taken aback, I don't know what to do. I immediately want to apologize to her again, but she doesn't want me to talk, so I just wait for it. Whatever she has to say to me, I deserve it.

"I thought we were in this together," she says. Her hands clench the steering wheel until her knuckles turn white. "It made it easier to get through everything because I knew you were going through the same stuff." She lets out a breath. "I'm not trying to diminish what you're going through. I know you're Brady's sister. I know you have a lot more history with him. He was your brother, but I thought we connected in that way." She pauses. "And then you left me…again."

I open my mouth to say something, but immediately shut it.

"You were in shock at the hospital. I was trying to get you help. That's why I went up to the nurse's station in the first place. When I turned around, you were gone. I tried to tell them you went back there, but they told me you must've slipped outside for some fresh air, but they don't know you like I know you. It started making sense after that. What you asked me on the way to the football game. Whether I would still want to fall for Brady if I knew what was going to happen to him. Once I remembered that, I knew you were going to leave, but you'd already done it. I get it. You were scared. I know you want to get the hell out of here, that all this place does is remind you of Brady. I feel the same way."

"I'm so sorry I—"

She holds up her hand. "I don't want your apologies. I have something to say to you." She swallows. "I didn't answer you properly when you asked me that question in the car...about whether I would still love Brady. The truth is, I didn't know what to say at the time. I'm too wrapped up in my own grief sometimes, like you, to know what to do or say. But I have an answer for you now. You asked me whether I'd still choose to be with Brady even knowing what would happen to him, and I'm telling you yes. Wholeheartedly, yes. Some of those moments with Brady were the best of my life." Tears track down her face. I want to reach over to hug her, but I can tell she needs to get this out. "I can't imagine not knowing what it means to love. But not just that, not knowing what it means to love Brady. His warm heart. His old soul. I'll probably love someone else again, but I won't ever love someone like I loved Brady. Not in depth or emotion, but because we're all different. I love you, but that's a different kind of love. I love my parents, but that's a different kind of love. I wouldn't want to miss out on any of it. So, I'm sorry, Briar. I didn't know what to say, which made you want to run away because you were scared. I'm telling you, it's worth it. It's worth every second. Even the fights and the angry words because that just makes the other times sweeter. You didn't have to run away from Reid, Briar. Even if something had happened to him, what little time you did have with him would've made all the heartache worth it."

What did I do to deserve friends like this? I reach out and hug her, holding her shaking body to me. I want to tell her how much that meant to me, but I know I'll just send us both into crying fits, and I don't want to do that. "Wow," I say through fractured vision. "That sounded really wise, Jules." I squeeze her once more and sit back. "It wasn't your fault I left though." I close my eyes, thinking back on seeing Reid in that bed.

"I don't know why I did. I can't explain it, really. But it wasn't you."

She opens up her glove compartment and pulls out a pack of tissues. "I just need you to know that it's worth it. I don't want you to be afraid of the relationship you have with Reid. And you shouldn't live it worrying that it's all going to get taken away either."

I nod. "I won't. I promise. So, you're not mad at me?"

She wipes her eyes and slices a look my way. "Don't push your luck. You still made me, and everyone else, worry about you. I just want you to know you don't have to do it again. The next time you leave Spring Hill should be when we're all going to college."

"If I ever catch up from this week," I say, dreading the amount of work I have in my backpack right now.

"Are you kidding me? You were at the top of the class. You can do it again." She shoos me out of the car. I hesitate, not wanting to leave her while she's upset, but she shakes her head. "I'll be fine, Briar. Just know that if you leave again, we're going to have real problems. Understand?"

I nod quickly, then get out of the car, pushing the door closed behind me. I climb the front steps and turn to wave at Jules as she backs out of the driveway. Once she's out of sight, I walk in, yelling out to Dad, "I'm home!"

I hear a muffled reply from inside his office, so I retreat to my room. If Mom was the one here, she probably would've been looking at Jules and I from the living room window, timing how long it took for me to get inside. Not that I don't deserve that because I do.

I tackle my worst subject first, getting it out of the way. There are two Science assignments, which takes me until dinner. My mom popped her head in when she got home from work to make sure I was there. She's still acting funny, not that I can blame her.

I thoroughly realize I fucked up.

When Dad gets me for dinner, the house smells amazing. I walk out to find that Mom's made her homemade pizza, my favorite. "Smells delicious," I say, my mouth already watering.

"We thought you'd like it," Mom says. She still seems stiff, yet making my favorite meal. Something seems up. Or, it's going to take her a while to warm up to me again. To gain her trust back, so she doesn't keep looking at me like I'm going to run out of the house at any moment. I already apologized to them, and honestly, I know that's not what they need. They just need me not to do it again.

When we settle down to eat, I try light conversation. I don't look at Brady's empty seat like I usually do. Instead, I tell them I caught up all of my Science work and will be starting on History after dinner.

The pizza is so delicious that I almost miss the look that transpires between my parents. It makes my stomach bottom out. My dad wipes his face with his napkin and sets it down. "Your mom and I have been talking about something."

"Okay..."

"We," he says, clearing his throat like he doesn't want to say we at all, but has to. My mom reaches over to grab his hand. "We think it's best if you actually did go stay at Grandma and Grandpa's. Until the end of the year."

My mouth drops. My mind tries to make connections on why they would be saying this, but instead, there's nothing but a hazy fog. "What?"

"We talked to the school closest to their house today. There's no problem there. They'll let you in, and you can start on Wednesday."

"But Grandma and Grandpa live in another state."

Dad opens his mouth to say something, but Mom cuts in. "We think it would be good for you to get some distance from here. That's what you've been trying to tell us, anyway. By running away."

"Maybe it would be better for you if you were in a

school that didn't remind you of Brady every day," my dad finally says.

"But I have friends here."

"Friends that you run away from."

"That's not fair."

"*That's* not fair?"

My dad squeezes her hand, and my mom cuts herself off. I look at both of them, but I can hardly believe these two are my parents right now. "You want to send me away?"

"You're not happy, Briar," Mom says, her voice laced in desperation. The emotion feels like a thick cloak over her words.

"But—"

"We want you to try it until the end of the school year," my dad says, smiling a little for me. "If you want to come back next year, you can. But we think you might actually like it there. You might actually want to stay for your Senior year too."

"What about Theo Laughlin?"

Mom and Dad exchange a look. "Who's Theo Laughlin?"

"Pretty much the only person who can beat me out for Valedictorian. Leaving now would mean he would win."

"Briar, let's get serious for a moment. The two

times you ran away is going to make this Theo guy win. Not moving you to Grandma and Grandpa's."

"I'm not going," I say, staring between the two.

Mom stands. A waft of pizza aroma hits me in the face and then it dawns on me why she made my favorite meal. They tried to make this as pleasing as possible. They want to send me away, and I'm just supposed to go along with it. Maybe they think that's what I want, but I can't imagine leaving the guys and Jules. And Reid. My God, not after what just happened at school.

"I'm not going," I say again. "I already promised I won't run away again, and I mean it. I don't know why I did it, okay? I don't know why I left, but it had nothing to do with wanting to get away from the memory of Brady or you or my friends. I was just scared."

My dad looks at my mom, his eyes almost pleading. Mom straightens her shoulders. "You are leaving, Briar. I'm taking you in the morning."

A sound comes from the hallway, and we all look up. "I can't let you do that."

Reid is standing in the entryway, his eyes glued to my mom's.

"Reid, come in," Mom says, turning on a smile like flipping a switch. "I made pizza."

Reid stares at me as he comes over. He places his hands on my shoulders. "I can't let you move Briar away from here," he says. His fingers dig into my skin, grounding me.

"Reid," my mom says, shaking her head. "None of this is your fault. It's just—"

"I can't let you take her away because I love her," he says. His voice rings through the house with finality. My mom's eyes widen as she looks between the two of us. Dad takes a sip of his milk, drowning any reaction I could have gleaned from him. "We're seeing each other. It happened while you were on vacation and there just hasn't been a good time since to tell you what was going on with us. I'm sorry."

"Well, this is...certainly surprising," Dad says.

"Briar can say all she wants that she doesn't know why she left, but I think I do. She saw me get hurt, and it reminded her of Brady. She came into the emergency room to see me, and when she did, it scared the crap out of her. She didn't want me to end up like Brady, so she just ran. I'm sure she won't do it again."

Reid gives me a squeeze, so I mimic him. "I won't do it again. I promise."

"Have a seat," Dad says, motioning toward Brady's chair. Reid doesn't take it. He takes the one next to me and puts his hand on my thigh. For the first time, I look over at him. Concern is etched into his features. He looks pale, too. I put my hand over his and hold him tightly in my grip.

"This doesn't really change anything," Mom says. "I think Briar could use a change of scenery."

"I don't want a change of scenery."

Mom's fingers tighten around the edge of the table. She looks like she's barely hanging on by a thread.

"Please," Reid says, desperation in his voice. "I need her."

From my peripheral, I see Dad look between the two of us, but my focus is on Reid's eyes. He looks so hurt. Pain is radiating from him, and all I really want to do is ask him what's going on.

"Your mom and I will do some more talking."

Mom starts to protest, but Dad gets up and gets Reid a plate. He brings it back from the kitchen, and we all finish eating in silence. It feels like it takes ages for Reid to eat. All eyes are on us. I can feel Mom teeming with things to say. When we finish, I drag Reid back to my room, telling them we'll be doing homework. The only thing she can get out is to keep the door open.

I do as she says, but pull him to the bed as soon as we get in there. "I'll talk to her," Reid says, staring back down the hallway as my parents pick up after dinner.

"Don't worry." He brings me toward him and kisses me on the top of the head.

"I'm not worried about that," I say to him. Maybe it's being naïve. Maybe I should be more worried about what my parents just said, but the only thing I'm worrying about right now is the look on Reid's face. He looks lost. "What happened at practice? Is everything okay?"

Reid takes my face in his hands. "What matters is that you're staying here. Don't worry."

I glower at him. "Reid Parker, tell me what happened at practice before I call Lex or Cade."

He drops his hand from my face and stands. He walks to the side of the room and leans against my desk. "Coach called me into his office." He pauses, his fingers tightening around the wood. After a moment, he shrugs. "He's starting Oscar next game."

9

I gasp. Who does this guy think he is? He just starts school one day and now he gets to be our starting quarterback? "Coach Jackson can't do that." I stand and step toward Reid, but he moves out of my touch.

"He doesn't have another choice, and besides, Coach says it's just until I get better." His eyes hold mine like he wants to believe Coach and he wants me to believe Coach, but there's a flicker of fear underneath. What if Oscar is just that good? What if Reid can't get better in time?

My brother and the guys all had plans to go to college together. Jules was going to follow Brady while I was just interested in going to the best college I could get into. Now, I'm not even at the top of my class anymore, Brady's dead, and Reid's no longer our starting quarterback. He can act like the tough guy all he wants, but I know this must be bothering him.

I march right up to him and grab his hands, lifting to my tiptoes. He checks the doorway behind me. "If your parents catch us this close…"

"Reid, be honest with me. You must be thinking about Warner's right now."

He blinks. "Last I heard, Oscar wanted to play there too."

I bite my lip to keep from showing any reaction.

"Now he's playing in my spot. Yes, I'm worried," he says, his voice hardening. "It's been all we talked about since we were little. I need to get into Warner's. I need the scholarship money."

I close my eyes, replaying snippets of conversation I've heard in the past. "The All-State Scholarship?"

Reid pulls out of my grasp and moves away again. "Yes, the All-State."

"You could still win it."

His eyes flare with emotion. "Not when I'm fucking sidelined!" His outburst makes me jump. He quickly looks toward the door and then lowers his voice. "I just can't talk about this right now, Briar. Okay? Are you going to be alright here for the night?" His gaze softens, and he finally moves toward me. He wraps his strong arms around me and kisses my temple. "If your mom starts talking about sending you off again, call me. I'll think of something."

I grip his shirt. "Don't think about me. I'm fine," I tell him, hoping I'm right. I'm hoping Mom just had a momentary lapse of judgment and that she really wouldn't send me to live a state away without them, without everyone. "You have enough on your plate."

He pulls away, his hand cupping my cheek as he turns my gaze to meet his. "I never have too much on my plate to worry about you, okay? Call me."

With that, he seals a short kiss to my lips and walks down the hallway. He passes Brady's door, giving it a solid look that makes me wonder what he's thinking right now. He probably feels like I did just after Brady died, seeing my life that I had laid out in front of me just crumble in front of my very eyes. It was like the very foundation I had counted on was now shaky and crumbling.

When I hear the front door shut, I message Lex and Cade. **Check on Reid, would you? I'm worried about him.**

I receive thumbs up in response. After that, I fall back on my bed. I want nothing more than to run after him, but I'm grounded, and there's no way I can get out of it. Not with my parents threatening to ship me off. I feel trapped, so my mind wanders. Just what in the hell does Sasha think she's doing? She dated Reid for years and now she's acting like he's her mortal enemy. She paid that Richards guy off to hurt him. Now she brings in his only true competition to the school he wants and the scholarship he needs.

I pick my phone back up and look through the old messages I sent to Ezra when I thought it was Ezra and not her, just looking for anything to be used against her. She needs to back off of Reid. And me.

I kind of want to haul off and kick her ass. Mar her pretty, cheerleader face. But I know that won't really hurt her. It would make me feel good for a few seconds. Really good. But I'm on thin ice as it is, so physical violence probably isn't a great idea. Also, I've never hit anyone before in my life. I make a fist with my hand, looking at it. I know I could do it if I had to, but it's not the revenge I want. I want Sasha to feel like this. I want her to suffer as much as we are right now. Whatever it is she wants, I want her to feel it keep moving out of her grasp like she'll never be able to achieve it.

That probably makes me all kinds of wrong, but I don't care.

Instead of working on History, I pull out a blank notebook and start making a list of what Sasha Pontine treasures in this life. At the top, I have her parents' approval. In my head, I can still see her face when I made them move at the football game. I can see the shame in their eyes when the crowd got on my side instead of theirs. On the next line, I write family legacy. In the other few lines, I fill it in with popular boyfriend, cheerleading, looks, admiration, basically anything I can think of.

Now, I just have to figure out any way I can to try to take these away from her. I've already started some of it. At least, Lex has. He placed the phone call to police. She'll never tell us what happened to her, if anything, when she got to the police station, but maybe we can find out and exploit it. If she got in trouble, any trouble at all, the best thing to do is to make sure everyone else knows because that's the exact kind of thing her family wouldn't want to get out.

I pick up the phone and text Lex privately. **How can we find out if Sasha got in trouble for the picture?**

I can ask... What do you have planned? Come over?

I know my parents probably won't like this, but I'll tell them Lex is going to help me catch up with my work. Instead, he's going to help me plot out revenge against the sadistic cheerleader. At the risk of sounding like a cheesy nineties flick, I can't wait to take her down.

I'll check on Reid first then I'll be over. See you then.

I put the phone down and walk out to the kitchen table where my parents are sitting and talking. Dad looks up first. "What's up, Sweetie?"

"Lex is coming over. He's going to help me decipher some of this work I have to do to catch up."

I stare at Mom, praying she won't bring up leaving again. She'd said we would leave tomorrow, but I'm just going to act as if I didn't hear that part. If I was changing schools, I wouldn't need to hand in the homework I missed. I hope this subtle hint tells her I'm serious about staying in Spring Hill.

Holy shit. I never thought I'd hear myself say those words again. I guess the Spring Hill Blues have lifted —for now.

10

The next morning when Reid picks me up to go to school, Mom and Dad aren't there. They weren't there when I got up either. All I got was a note that said they had to go into the office early. Part of me cheered inside because at least I knew I wasn't going to have to fight my mom this early in the morning about staying in Spring Hill.

I dropped a bagel into the toaster for him and carried it out when I heard him pull into the driveway. When I get out there, though, it's Lex in his silver Honda Civic waiting for me, not Reid. He gets out of the car before he notices I'm on the front step. When he glances up, he pauses with his hand on the door. He must see my questioning gaze because he automatically explains, "Reid got a doctor's appointment first thing this morning."

"Oh," I say. I pull out my phone to check to see if he'd sent me a message, and he hadn't.

I fret over my lip, but Lex walks up to me. "He got a last-minute opening. He had to take it."

"Right," I say, smiling for him. "Well, here, this is for you then." I hand him the bagel.

Lex takes it from me and gives me a thin-lipped smile. "Thanks. So, I called the police station this morning to talk to the same guy I reported the picture to. He couldn't tell me much, but he did say that she was assigned community service."

My eyebrows raise and a grin pulls at my lips. "Seriously?"

He nods. "He didn't say so, but she probably had to pay a fine too. I did some research last night on the internet after I left your house," he explains.

"I wish we could get a hold of the police report. That would be awesome. Her parents would die if something like that came out." I take a seat in Lex's car with a huge smile on my face. This was better news than I thought. I'd completely imagined that Sasha didn't get anything but a stern talking to, but this is epic. This is definitely something we can use against her to keep her from messing with Reid, or hell, even as payback for what she's already done. She deserves this and a hell of a lot more.

Lex starts the car and uses the mirrors to back out of the driveway before pointing the car toward school and taking a bite out of Reid's bagel. "I wish we had that. I was also thinking maybe we could get lucky and figure out where she's doing the community service. If we got pictures of her there..."

"She could lie," I say. "If she's doing community service somewhere, she could just say it's for her college applications. Damn. I really wish we had the police report."

Lex side-eyes me from the driver's seat. "I haven't seen you this worked up about something since Theo Laughlin took you out of the number one spot." When I glare over at him, he holds his hands up defensively. "Still a sore subject. Got it."

"She really needs to pay for what's happened, Lex," I tell him, justifying in my mind why I want to publicly humiliate this awful excuse for a human being. "She thinks she's untouchable, but she's not. Remember when she told Reid that Spring Hill was her school, not his. This is just a struggle for power. My God, we have a freaking Stalin on our hands. In high school. Imagine what she's going to be like out of school." I shake my head. "It's not right."

"I completely agree," Lex says. He's quiet for a moment as we pass the early morning crowd on the streets. There are adults going to work and other students just like us, making their way to Spring Hill High where they don't even know the lengths some people will go to. "I just don't want you to lose yourself, Briar."

I shrug. "I'm just trying to protect the ones I care about. Isn't that what you three tried to do for me?"

His fingers tighten around the steering wheel. I know I've struck a nerve, which is fine by me. It was meant to. I don't need to be coddled anymore. Right now, shit's happening to Reid, and I won't stand for it.

When we pull into the school, Cade's waiting for us. He jogs up to the car as we get out. "Any word?"

Lex shakes his head. "I don't even think he's gone in yet. He'll text."

I grit my teeth, but in the next moment, I try to make myself relax and not worry about the fact that I'm apparently the last person to know that Reid went to the doctor this morning. I shouldn't be bitter about that. At all. Right?

"Hey," a voice says.

The three of us look up to find Oscar without his arm candy. He hikes his bag up on his shoulder. "Reid around?"

Lex practically growls at him. I'm right there with him.

Oscar looks annoyed. "He ran out of practice before I could talk to him."

"I'm pretty sure he doesn't have shit to say to you, Drego," Cade sneers. "You should go back to Rawley Heights."

"Please," Oscar says. "No one wants to be at Rawley Heights, least of all me. You know we don't get the same opportunities there. I did what anyone would do in my position."

"Well, you better be careful," I tell him. "Sasha could turn on you quick. Look what happened to Reid."

His cocky grin smooths out a bit. He doesn't exactly look like he's quaking in his boots, but he should be. He probably has no idea she's the reason why he can even come to this school to play for Spring Hill. She got rid of our quarterback, and she needed someone to replace him.

"You should watch yourself."

"Thanks for the warning, Partner," I deadpan.

Lex and Cade both move in front of me. Oscar laughs as he walks away, shrugging like he couldn't care less what's going on.

"Partner?" Cade asks.

"We got paired together on an English assignment because we were the only ones not around when everyone partnered up."

"Reid's going to fucking hate that," Cade says, letting out a breath.

"I tried to get out of it."

"Let's just let Reid worry about recovering. When he does that, none of this other shit will matter."

"It makes me wonder," I say, watching Oscar's retreating back. He's been here only two days, and he already acts like the king of the school. "Why would Oscar even come here if he thought Reid would get better and take his spot back?"

Cade runs a hand through his dark hair. "It's like he said, Rawley Heights doesn't get much attention, even if they do have a really good quarterback. Spring Hill has the legacy players. Not to mention that Oscar's the star of the show in Rawley Heights. They don't have the draw like we do here. Our whole team is good, so it makes us—Reid—look even better. Scouts want to see that foundation and teamwork. Oscar's guys can barely run a buttonhook."

"So, he wasn't lying then? About no one wanting to be in Rawley Heights?"

Lex and Cade fix me with a look. "Don't go feeling

sorry for him, Briar," Cade says. "What he did was dirty, and he knows it."

We start walking toward the school. "What do the other guys on the team think about it?"

"They feel bad for Seven, but what can we all do?" Lex asks. "Coach made the call. There are other guys who are hoping for college scouts too. Barnhardt won't bring the scouts in, but Drego will."

"I guess we just have to make sure Reid gets better," I say. Already, I feel my mind drifting. When we get to my locker, I pull out my cell and text Reid, telling him I hope he's okay and to let me know when he's done. I continue on to homeroom with my fingers crossed that we'll get good news today instead of the onslaught of bad news we've been wading through recently.

―――

Notes get thrown at me all day long with snide comments about my breasts. I'd be embarrassed, but I can't think about much more than Reid. I check my phone in between classes, but I haven't heard anything yet, which makes my mind dwell on negative things. I'm too caught up in my own head that I don't see Oscar blocking the path to English, and I run right into him. He steadies me on my feet, and when I look up, I growl. "Christ, Oscar. What are you doing?"

"What am I doing? You ran into me."

I grit my teeth. He looks down at me with a smug smile that I really wish I could wash off his face.

I try to push past him into the room, but he stops me. "Mr. Shaver approved us to work in the library today, so we can do research on our project."

I glare up at him. "I didn't ask Mr. Shaver to work in the library."

He smiles broadly like he's the king and I'm his disciple. "I did."

I really wish I could tell him to get fucked, but my gaze rests on Theo. If I really do want to prove to my parents and myself that I'm better now, I need to go after my old goals, which means I need to get a good grade on this project, whether Oscar is my partner or not. "Fine," I grumble.

We turn and start to walk down the hall toward the library. "Wow. Has anyone told you you have some amazing social skills?"

"Has anyone told you that not everyone has to smile just for your pleasure?"

I can feel him peek at me while we walk down the hallway, but he doesn't say anything. When we enter the library, I find the first free table and sit while he walks a pass from Mr. Shaver to the librarian. I pull out a notebook and am already making notes in it when he drops his book bag down on the wooden table. It makes a loud thunk, and I freeze before staring up at him. He, again, looks at me like he could give a shit. I guess there are some people in this world who are just like that. They don't care about the amount of noise they make, just that they're being seen or heard. To them, it's not about the noise, it's about the attention.

I shake my head and finish writing down my initial thoughts. When he sits, I say, "I figure we should tackle the different themes. I can work on pulling research for one, and you can work on another. How does that sound?"

He shrugs, barely even listening to me. Well, he could be listening to me, but his attention is on everything else in the library but me. He's casually looking at all the other students in here, the librarian, even the bookshelves.

"You did want to work on this, right?" I ask. "That's why you asked to come down here, correct?"

Oscar slowly tracks his gaze back to me. He has deep brown eyes that are almost black. "I like you, Briar." I must make a disgusted face because he laughs. "I know, beyond all reason. You certainly haven't earned it."

"I wasn't looking to earn it, jackass."

His face flushes. "What's your problem with me, anyway? You and your posse of three there are the only ones who can't stand me since I got here."

"That's probably the dumbest fucking question I've ever heard. Why do you think we wouldn't like you?"

He scowls. "Listen, I have to do what I have to do. I'm a man of opportunity and the opportunity fell in my lap. So, I'm not supposed to try to make my life better just because I might hurt someone else's feelings? Get real. That's not the way the world works, and if you think it does, you're naïve. Or a child. Some of us had to grow up at a young age."

Fury simmers underneath the surface. "You don't think I know about growing up early? A dead brother will do that to you, so watch where you act all self-righteous."

I stand up from the table, my chair gliding over the threadbare carpet as I head to the stacks. I search for The Great Gatsby, find two copies, and come back, dropping one paperback in front of him. He dribbles his fingers over the cover. "Listen, I'm sorry. I'm sure it sucked to lose Brady. I didn't mean to discount that. But don't discount my shit either."

Ignoring him, I open up my copy. I flip through the

pages, not reading, but like I can somehow transfer all the words into my brain to try to find the themes with just a glance even though I know that's not possible. I'm going to have to do some searching. I've watched the movie and enjoyed it, but I probably don't have enough time to read the book, research the paper, and write it. Oscar will probably be no help on those fronts either.

"So, uh, I know why people have been saying shit about your chest." My face flames. I peek up to find him staring, but when he sees me looking at him looking at me, he glances away. "It's pretty fucked up, if you ask me."

"Yeah, well, that's who you've aligned yourself with. Congratulations, Oscar. You've got yourself a winner."

My mind races, but underneath the anger building inside me of Sasha still showing people the picture and telling people what she did, I know I still need to figure out a way to get to her. I look up at Oscar to find he looks somewhat troubled. Odd, considering he's a man of opportunity like he said. Could what Sasha be doing really bother him? It seems unlikely.

"Did she show you?"

His jaw hardens, and I see a muscle pop. "Yeah, I told her she should knock it off. It's not cool."

"A lot of other people disagree," I say, commenting on the fact that I can barely move down the hallway now without guys leering at me. It's disturbing.

"Yeah, well, people can be assholes."

"Maybe they're just men of opportunity too."

He stops staring down at the cover of the book and flicks his gaze to me. A smile pulls at my lips because I know I've struck a chord with him. He goes back to inspecting the cover and says, "I thought you might want to know that she's being punished. Her parents had to pay a five thousand dollar fine, and she's got to do some community service for the parks system or something like that."

My stomach squeezes. This is exactly the information we wanted. "How do you know that?" I ask. I fail at trying to seem uninterested, but I hope it just comes across as wanting to get revenge on her because I do want to get revenge on her. In the worst way.

He shrugs. "I was over at her house, and I heard her parents yelling at her. They're super pissed." He chuckles a little, then gets serious again. He shrugs. "I thought it might help to know that."

"What's curious is why she would keep showing people the picture if it really bothered her that she was being punished."

"I guess she's a woman of opportunity," Oscar says, a dare in his eyes.

"The perfect couple," I say, oozing the words with sarcasm.

Oscar and I don't talk for the rest of the period.

11

On my way to lunch, I finally get a text from Reid, asking me to meet him outside the men's locker room. I do as he asks. I wait for a few minutes, glancing down at my phone screen as the time ticks by to the start of lunch. Just as the bell starts to ring, a hand reaches out from behind the men's locker room door and slides around my wrist. He pulls, and I go with him willingly.

With a firm hold, he moves through the locker room. We pass rows of lockers, but he doesn't bother to turn around once. I'm about to ask him where we're going when I see a door in the back of the room. He opens it and steps inside, moving me in behind him.

When the door shuts, it's pitch black inside. I can't

see anything. All I have is his hand is mine. "Reid, are you okay?"

"I need you," he says. His voice is guttural, bare, like he's holding onto the edge of a cliff and his grip is slipping.

"What is it?"

His lips land hard on mine. He kisses me until he takes my breath away. His mouth is punishing, kicking up wave after wave of need as it batters against me. His hand moves over my hip then up under my shirt where it settles on the bare skin of my ribs. The skin underneath his touch radiates warmth and turns into an inferno when he moves up, grasping my breast in his palm. "Whoever calls these anything but the most beautiful breasts is lying."

My body hums under his touch. I admit, when we told my parents we were dating, I was wondering how we were going to do this. How we were still going to be free to explore each other. I love this idea. I love it a lot. "I missed you," I say, meaning it wholeheartedly.

"God, I missed you," he groans, kneading my breasts in his rough palms. "Tell me this is a stupid idea."

I push up on my tiptoes to lay a scorching kiss to his mouth, telling him exactly what I think of this idea. His already hard cock turns to stone against my thigh and he groans. His hands tease the hem of my shirt, and then he pulls it over my head. He pushes against me until my back hits what I assume is the door behind us. His hips work into me until I'm breathing heavy. I lower my hands, fumble with his jeans until I push them to the ground. He unclasps my bra, pulls the straps down my shoulders, and I don't see where it lands, but I feel his hot breath on my nipple right before his mouth closes around it. I let out a muffled cry until my hand finds his dick. I work him right through his boxers. His body shudders, then he lifts his head to my forehead. We breathe each other's breath.

"Do you want to stop?"

"No."

He kisses my lips, then bends. I don't know what he's doing until I hear the crinkly sound of what I can only assume is a condom package. "Take your pants off, Briar." His husky voice does things to me. I don't hesitate. I unclasp my button, force the zipper down and peel my jeans and panties off. It's so dark, I don't see him. For a moment, I feel alone, standing at the edge of a room, naked, but then I feel his warmth as he steps close to me and the feeling of safety slides over my skin.

He kisses me again, and I open my mouth for him, forcing us to tease each other. His hands hook around my thighs and lift. I make a surprised cry when he lifts me off the ground, and I automatically hook my feet behind him for safety, but in the next moment, I'm not even thinking about that. I'm thinking about him pressed against my core. "Reid," I breathe out.

He pushes forward until he slides inside, resting there with a loud groan. "I love you," he tells me, right before he starts moving inside.

We start out slow, testing and feeling, until the sensations become too much. I can't get close enough to him. I can't feel enough, and those same thoughts are ricocheted back on me when his movements quicken. The door thumps behind us with the thrust of his hips. My legs tighten around him. "Reid, oh my God."

His hand sneaks between us, flicking over my clit until my orgasm hits fast and hard. His mouth covers mine the moment it hits, eating up all my release until he finishes with a flurry, diving inside me before moaning long and hard when his dick jerks. His breath stutters out of him.

I reach up to touch his cheek, then kiss him, solidifying this moment for the two of us. He steps back, guiding me to the floor again. For a moment, I just stand there while I hear him pull the condom off. His arms wrap around me a moment later. "I'm going to die if we can't get your parents to ease up on you being grounded. I need you right now."

"I'll talk to my parents."

Reid laughs, and I know he's trying to tell me that the chances of them listening to me are nil. He helps me dress, handing me my clothes in the dark. "I don't think that'll help any. You're the reason you got yourself grounded in the first place."

He's got a point there. "You really think you can sweet talk my parents, don't you?"

"I sweet-talked you, didn't I?"

I pull him toward me once I'm dressed, sealing a kiss to his lips. I miss this Reid. The intense but sweet one I always knew he was. I hate to see him so worried about things that are out of his control. "So, you went to the doctor this morning?"

I hear him putting his own clothes on, the sound of his zipper zippering ending our encounter. He opens the door, and when a shaft of light filters in, I notice he already has both of our bags in his hand. He looks out, making sure there's no one in the room and then leads me into the locker room once again. "I'm sorry I didn't tell you. I didn't want to worry you."

"You know that doesn't work, right?"

He hands me my bag with a soft smile.

"Well?" I ask again. "What did he say?"

His lips thin. "He doesn't want me playing yet. The hit was so hard he wants to keep monitoring me.

He told me there are a bunch of cases where people with head injuries have gone back into it too soon, and he doesn't want me to be a statistic."

"We don't want that, either," I say, thinking of Brady. I don't think he had any head injuries before he had the aneurysm, but it's possible he did.

He seems to sense my line of thinking because he wraps his hand around mine, squeezing my fingers. "I'm going to listen to the doctor, but," he hesitates, ending his sentence with a growl. "You want to get out of here? I just want to be alone with you."

He sneaks his head outside the locker room door to see if anyone's in the hallway. He pulls me outside, and we stand there, looking at one another. The question is still in his eyes. I don't even hesitate. "Sure."

A grin overtakes his face. We start walking toward the side door. We're almost there when a voice carries down the hallway toward us. "Where are you guys going?"

I look around to find Cade and Lex in the mouth of the cafeteria.

Lex looks over at me. "You can't afford anymore absences, Briar."

I open my mouth to tell him to screw school when Reid sighs. "He's right," he whispers. "I don't know what I was thinking."

"It's okay," I tell him.

He shakes his head. "No, it's not."

"Thanks for calling us when you were done, fucker," Cade says as both he and Lex move down the hallway toward us. "What did the doc say?"

Reid shakes his head, and the two boys' looks turn solemn. "Next time," Lex says. "I'm sure he'll approve you next time."

"When do you go back?" I ask.

"A week," Reid says. His voice is thin, like it's tethered to reality by the barest of threads. The encounter in the locker room, wanting to leave, I understand all of it. I just wish we hadn't been interrupted because I understand that, sometimes, all you need is to just get away for a little while.

"Come on," Cade says. "You guys should get some food." He gives me a once-over. "And you might want to run your hands through your hair, Briar, unless you want everyone to know you just had sex."

My face flames. I immediately run my hands through my long strands a few times while Reid grins at me. "How?" I ask, looking at Cade.

"Sex hair? It's a thing."

I groan under my breath but follow them into the cafeteria. Jules looks up, a smile flitting over her face when she sees both Reid and I accompanying the other two in. She gives a knowing look and then peppers Reid with questions about his doctor's appointment as Cade goes to get us something to eat. After Reid answers all her questions, Lex says, "Oscar wanted to talk to you this morning. Heads up."

Reid's jaw ticks.

I look behind me to the other table and notice Oscar and Sasha aren't there. "They left a few minutes ago," Jules says, just as Cade gets back to the table with a tray filled with food.

"I got paired up with Oscar for an English assignment," I say, clearly expressing my disappointment on the matter. "We were working in the library, and he told me he heard a fight between Sasha and her parents. He told me she got fined five thousand dollars and has to do community service for the local parks service for having that picture."

Everyone's silent for a moment as they take the information in, but Jules finally says, "She should've gotten worse. Five thousand dollars is nothing to her parents."

Lex and I exchange a look. What he'd heard from the officer this morning was true. For a second, I wonder if we can use Oscar to spread the rumor about the punishment she got, but it's doubtful he would go against Sasha. He'd probably outright deny it. He is a man of opportunity after all. I tell the group as much and they agree.

Reid casts a look between Lex and me. He finishes off a slice of pizza and wipes his hand on a napkin. "So, your plan is to get back at her, huh?"

"She hurt you," I say, daring him to disagree with me. "She's not getting away with that."

"It's not going to be easy. If you think she's bad, her parents are worse."

"I just want to show her that she's not as untouchable as she thinks she is. She manipulates everything," I say, making sure I whisper the words instead of yelling them. "She got you hurt. She got you replaced on the team. She pretended to be my friend. I mean, what the hell is her problem?"

"She ruins anyone who gets in her way," Reid says. "She's always been like that."

When I look at him, I still can't believe he was with her for so long. If he knew she was like this, what was the appeal? It makes my skin crawl.

"Don't look at me like that," he says finally. After a beat, he looks away. I can tell he's embarrassed, upset even, about their relationship.

It doesn't matter now. We can't change what's in the past.

"If we really want to get to her, all we have to do is

take away her power and prestige," Cade suggests.

"We need to find physical proof of her community service," Lex says, repeating the conclusion we came to earlier in the car. "A police report, a write-up, anything proving what she got community service for. Then, we'll tell everyone."

"We're not bringing Briar down with her," Reid says, anger lacing his words. He looks at all of us. "I don't like the idea. Going after her confirms you were the one in the picture."

"Everyone at the school knows it's me anyway," I tell him.

I'd already thought of this. If I want to take Sasha down about having my picture, I might get tangled up in the messy wake, but I'm willing to take the risk. If what Oscar says is true and her parents are already furious at her, it won't take much to drag her down.

Reid shakes his head. "We should go after the guy who hit me instead. He's fucking scum. We should be able to get him to out her for what she did to me."

"Then it's just a he said she said."

Reid shrugs. "Not if we have physical evidence. It can't hurt to try."

I reach out to rub his forearm. He's still trying to keep me safe, and I love him for it. But we're beyond that. Her shit isn't going to fly anymore.

12

That Friday is another game in the Spring Hill books that Reid doesn't play in. This time, though, he's actually on the sidelines, and I'm in the bleachers, watching him sit there with his sexy suit on while he observes the game he loves pass him by.

I try not to notice, but Oscar is good. Spring Hill wins because of him, and I can feel the conflicting emotions firing on Reid's face when he gets up to congratulate all the sweaty players when they jog off the field with the last seconds of the clock ticking down.

Sasha runs up to Oscar now, instead of Reid, planting a disgusting, triumphant kiss on him that turns my stomach. To all the world, she appears to be a happy cheerleader congratulating her boyfriend, but to those of us who know what she did to obtain all this, she looks like a playboy devil. She took out Reid, injuring him. He could've been hurt worse. I wonder if she ever thought of that. As if that wasn't enough, she invited Oscar to SHH, orchestrating Oscar's mother's new job at one of her father's companies and giving them a place to live.

Coach leads the team into the locker rooms, and I stay right where I am, casually watching as everyone else makes their way back to the parking lot. "You okay?" Jules asks, bumping into me.

I was surprised she came today, but I think she did it for both Reid and me, pushing down her emotions about Brady to be able to help us if we needed it. I shrug. "I guess. I just wonder how she can live with herself. It's disgusting."

"It takes a truly special person to be that much of a bitch."

"You're not kidding," I say.

Both mine and Jules's cell phones buzz at the same time. I take it out first, opening up the group text to find Cade telling us we're all going to the after party at Sasha's house. Before I can ask why in the hell we would do that, he texts, **Might find some shit.**

I blow out a breath. "I hope Reid is okay with this."

When Jules doesn't answer, I look over. "Are you going to come?"

She nods. "Yeah, I'm up for it. Who knew a little revenge would make me feel better?" She tries to carry it off as a joke, but I can still see the sadness just under the surface of her pale skin. I can feel my own too, hovering there, just waiting for me to get a break in my life to feel it all again. She smiles to herself. "I keep telling myself that Brady hated her, so he'd probably approve."

I laugh. "He hated her that much?"

She smirks. "He told me it made him want to hurl every time he saw Reid and Sasha together."

"It's so weird," I muse. "I wonder why he was so against Reid and me then. You know, if he really didn't like Sasha..."

"He'd probably rather watch Sasha and Reid suck face than his sister and his best friend," Jules says, quirking an eyebrow at me.

She's got a point there. But it still bothers me why Brady wouldn't have wanted us together. I'm just curious. It doesn't change my mind about him. Nothing would change my mind, but it would be an insight into what he was thinking. Plus, Reid is still a little unsure sometimes, so if Brady's reason was nothing big, it would put him at ease.

Jules stands and holds her hand out to me. "Come on, let's go get ready for this party."

I start to follow her down the bleachers, but I stop. "Shit. My parents aren't going to let me go to a party. They barely let me come here. They only did because Reid asked them."

My phone rings. I show Jules the screen when I see "Mom" scrolling across it. I swipe the screen to answer. Holding it up to my ear, I say, "Hey."

"I've agreed, but I swear to God, Briar, if you make your father and I worry about you again, I'm going to— Well, I don't know, but I do know you'll be on your way to Grandma and Grandpa's tomorrow. I'm not joking. You understand?"

"I—" I stumble over my words, not knowing what to say.

"That goes the same if I hear you were with anyone else but Reid. Okay?"

Now *that* I can answer. I don't want to hang out with anyone else but Reid. Well, Reid and the rest of our friends. "Yes, Mom. I promise. You don't have to worry."

"You don't deserve this, you know?"

My heart pounds heavily in my chest. She's right. "I know."

She sighs, and then the phone cuts out. I look at

Jules. I should be smiling right now because I get to go to the party, but I don't feel like this is a win at all. My parents—well, my mom—is still super pissed at me. Rightfully so. "I guess I'm going."

"How the hell did you do that?" Jules asks. "Your parents are usually strict."

"Reid," I say, shrugging. "Mom must've really appreciated everything he did for them after Brady died."

"Yeah. He was pretty great. Especially with you." She hip bumps me.

"Yeah, yeah," I say, remembering how mad I was when they started to work their way back into my life. I didn't like anyone. Except for Jules, of course. I just wanted to be left alone.

I'm so glad they didn't listen.

"Your parents won't care?" I ask.

"Are you kidding? They'll probably be thrilled I'm getting out of the house. They still keep looking at me like I'm going to break." She cuts herself off. "Not that I mind. My parents have been wonderful throughout all this. Really."

While we walk, she takes out her phone and types out a text to her mom. I watch as the response comes back within a minute. She slides her phone into her pocket, and we stop by Brady's memorial. "We really need to get some flowers in here or something. These wood chips are just too blah."

"Hey," a voice sounds from behind us. Jules and I immediately freeze because it's not from any voice we're expecting to hear. "It's nice what the school did for him, huh?"

I turn to stare at Oscar.

When neither one of us respond, he asks, "Are you guys going to the party?" He winks at me. "It would probably piss Sasha off."

I can feel the heat of Jules's gaze on me as she looks between us. "Yeah," I finally say. "We're going."

"Well, this ought to be interesting."

A smirk crosses his face before he jogs off to a car beeping in the parking lot. I recognize a few of the girls from the cheerleader squad in the car and wonder if Sasha is hiding in the backseat.

"Why the hell is he always talking to you?" Jules asks. "It's so weird."

"He says he likes me even though I'm not winning any social skills awards."

Instead of laughing, she narrows her eyes. "He likes you?"

"I'm sure he just meant likes me like a friend. Or as an acquaintance. We are working on that English project together." The one that's actually going pretty smoothly despite my original misgivings. It turns out Oscar doesn't mind putting in the hard work either.

"He better hope that's all it is or someone will have something to say about that."

That someone comes up behind Jules. I wave at Reid, who's dressed more casually now. I study him as he approaches. Head injuries are so weird because despite the disappearing mark on his forehead, no one would know the doctors are worried about his brain. He just looks normal, like he could go out there and play right now, which is probably why he's so frustrated.

"Hopefully, that's the last fucking time you have to watch a game from the sidelines," Cade tells him.

His words meet us before they actually do. When Reid gets there, I pop up on my tiptoes and give him a kiss. "I agree with Cade."

"Finally," Cade says, a hint of humor in his voice. "No one ever says that about me."

"We'll take my car," Reid says, ignoring us both. "It'll fit all of us better. You're good to go, right, Jules?"

She nods. "Mom doesn't mind as long as I'm not out too late."

"I had to promise the same thing to Pam, so we're good."

"Oh, Pam, huh? Is that how it is?" I tease, referencing his relationship with my mom.

"Yeah," he says, grinning. "You're welcome."

"Thank you," I say, truly meaning it. I squeeze his hand. At least my mom trusts him since she doesn't trust me right now.

Within a half hour, we're at Sasha's house. As soon as I see the front entrance, I second guess what the hell we're doing. I hate this girl. I feel like this is walking into her evil lair, but we have to be close to her to find the evidence we need.

Cade's friend Hayley is at the door when we walk up. I don't think they're as close as they were a few weeks ago, but apparently she and Cade are close enough that she agrees to let us into the party. I'm sure when Sasha sees us, she'll have something to say about that.

It strikes me then that no matter where the parties are at, they're the same thing over and over again. People stick with who they know, talking, drinking, and dancing all night. People rarely intersect with another group, and when they do, it's a shock. Or they're drunk out of their minds.

Reid holds me close to his side. Being near him helps soothe me, especially when we're here. This house reminds me so much of the type of person Sasha is. It's like it holds monstrous, terrible secrets. Sure, it's pretty on the outside, and the facade of the interior is made up like a showroom, but that's all it is. A giant, designer piece to hide the ugly.

Unlike other parties, our first stop isn't where the alcohol is. Reid's not allowed to have any alcoholic drinks right now, so the rest of us abstain for other reasons. Me? I want to be sharp tonight. Make sure I'll see Sasha coming if she does.

"I think I'm usually drunk at these," Jules grumbles as we all hide out in a corner.

I laugh. She's so right. This is a whole different lens to see things through.

"I'll make sure you're okay if you want to drink," Cade says. He holds up his hand like he's giving scout's honor.

All of us look at him. I start to smirk, but there's not a hint of insincerity in his words.

"Thanks," Jules says. "But, I'm good."

Cade looks away, watching everyone around us. I follow his gaze. A lot of the football guys are really partying it up tonight. The last few weeks without Reid were a bummer, or so I've learned. Now that they have a halfway decent quarterback back in the lineup, the mood is a lot happier. I turn to look at Reid, hoping being here around everyone celebrating the win he wasn't a part of isn't bothering him when from the corner of the dance floor, I see Oscar lead a stumbling Sasha to the center. She does one of her sexy tease dances, which looks a lot less polished than I'm sure she thinks it does due to her inebriated state. I look away, rolling my eyes. Oscar seems to be only half paying attention to her, but apparently, he finds something more interesting over in our group.

She follows his stare, and before I know it, a high-pitched, shriek cuts through the air. "What are you doing here?"

I close my eyes and breathe out. I don't even need to look to know they're coming this way. I was expecting this to happen. When I open my eyes, it's not exactly all of us she's looking at, it's me. And maybe Reid.

"This is a football after party," she sneers. Her gaze tracks up the arm Reid has around my waist, following it up to his face. "And you don't even play football anymore."

My blood boils. She can do what she wants to me, but not Reid. I step forward, and Reid's hand tightens around me, but it turns out, I don't even get to say anything.

"I invited them," Oscar says, his voice cutting through the crowd. "Parker's still on the team, Sash."

Sash? Ugh. Pet names for someone like her are just gross.

"For now," Sasha says, her scowl turning into a smile. Her lips lift too high at the corners so that she looks like a Cheshire cat.

I pull my hand from Reid's grip and move forward, shoving Sasha hard. She stumbles back into Oscar's chest. His hands go around her to keep her from falling, but I'm right in her face. "Hurt him again, and see what happens," I threaten. My hands turn to fists. I'm not a violent person usually, but maybe the guys are rubbing off on me.

Sasha starts to struggle out of Oscar's grip, but he holds on. When I look at him, his eyes are shining in excitement. "That was hot," he mouths.

A hand falls on my shoulder. Oscar looks up, narrows his eyes, and then drags Sasha away. I lean into the hand, but when I turn, I realize it was Lex who followed after me. I pull away slightly and look at him.

He lifts his hand from my shoulder, and I return to the group, each of them standing there with their eyebrows raised. Reid's eyeing Lex though, the area between his eyes pulling together in concentration as Jules gives me a beaming smile. "I like feisty Briar. She's fun, and that was long overdue."

"Feisty Briar's got balls," Cade agrees, raising his hand to give me a high five.

I reluctantly give him one even though my face warms in embarrassment and probably a bit of pride.

After he pulls away, his eyes round. "Holy. Shit," he growls.

I turn to follow his stare and immediately recognize who's stumbling through the party right now. My stomach bottoms out.

"Where's Sasha?" the guy calls out, voice slurring. "I need to find her."

I've seen him both in and out of his football pads, and each time, he looks like a piece of shit. The kind of guy who would take someone out for money or sex or any other damn thing Sasha promised him.

"That mother fucker," Lex says.

Reid looks on. He doesn't immediately get who it is, but I happen to look when it clicks into place. "That's him?" When no one answers, he looks at me and asks again with murder is in his eyes.

13

"Sasha!" Richards yells again.

He looks totally distraught. A lot less cocky than the previous times I've seen him. My body burns with the memory, and I shiver.

Behind me, Reid springs into action. Lex and Cade, both alert, move after him. Cade gets to the guy first while Lex gets to Reid. Jules grabs my hand, and we run after them. We sprint down a hallway while Reid yells expletives. My heart is in my throat. I don't know what the guys have planned, but eventually, we end up in an empty garage bay.

"The fuck?" the guy says.

His eyes are half-lidded. When Cade spins him around to face Lex and Reid, the guy squints. Recognition flickers in his eyes in about thirty seconds, a muted response time if you ask me, considering the waves of hostility floating off the guys in front of him.

The guy lifts his hand in the air. "She made me do it."

"You piece of shit," Reid roars.

I flick between the two of them. On one hand, I'm sure Reid really wants revenge on this guy for taking football away from him, but on the other, I don't want him to get hurt again. Lex stands cautiously nearby, moving between the two as I do.

"She told me you broke her heart."

That bitch doesn't have a heart.

"She told me you cheated on her, and that she just wanted you to pay. I swear, I didn't try to hit you that hard. I didn't know you were going to get seriously injured. I was just trying to send you a message for her."

Reid marches up to him until the guy backs up against a pillar in the middle of the garage. His nostrils flare, and Jules and I move around the room to watch. "You think I give a fuck about the hit? Listen here, motherfucker, if you go anywhere near Briar again, I'll kill you."

The guy's head rears back. He smacks it into the pillar behind him, dazing himself for a moment.

I gasp at his words, and the guy looks lazily over at me. Recognition flares in his eyes. "Shit," he mumbles.

"Yeah," Reid says. He places his forearm on the guy's neck and leans in. The guy clasps it, though not trying to move it at the moment. "Do you understand me? If you even so much as look at her, I'll tear your nuts off myself. You think women deserve to be treated that way? You think Sasha's somehow going to want you once she gets what she needs out of you? Fuck that."

"It was just supposed to be a prank," the guy says. "I thought—"

Reid leans into him, and he chokes. His face turns red while Reid just glares at him, keeping pressure on his throat. "Do we understand each other?"

He chokes again, but nods his head emphatically.

Mercifully, Reid leans away. The guy immediately clasps his hands around his throat. He wheezes in and out a few times. "I'm not doing any more for that cunt, anyway. She told her parents I got rough with her. They almost had my ass thrown in jail."

Reid moves away, coming toward me. His muscles are still locked up. I want to make sure he's okay, but at the same time, this guy was in on what happened. He could help us. I sneak past Reid to stand in front of Richards. "I need you to speak up about what you did to Reid. I need you to tell everyone what Sasha made you do."

The guy looks away, basically looking anywhere but at me. I roll my eyes when I realize what he's doing. Reid told him if he so much as looked at me, he was going to end him. Apparently in his drunken state, this is his solution to that.

"Please," I beg.

"Are you kidding me? I just told you her parents almost had me thrown in jail. I'm not fucking with her anymore. I came here tonight to tell her how much of a fucking bitch she is, but that's it."

"You owe us," I growl. "You hit Reid so hard, he got a fucking concussion. You were going to take pictures of me naked."

A rumbling comes from behind me. The guy tears his gaze off the ceiling and looks over my left shoulder and pales.

"I'm sorry," he says. He sneaks around me, raising his hands in the air like he's about to get arrested. "I am, but I'm done with this shit." When he gets closer to the door, he takes off. We can hear his footsteps thud against the tile as he runs down the hall.

Cade laughs. "I think that guy is about to piss his pants."

I groan, staring at the empty doorway. We had a

shot there, but nothing. The guy isn't anything but a coward with terrible excuses for his behavior. Even if he did tell everyone what happened, no one would probably believe him.

"Come on," Cade says, walking toward the doorway back to the party. "We should try to salvage the night."

We all start walking toward the door, but I pull back on Reid's hand after he slips it into mine. He's stiff at first, but when he turns toward me, he shifts back to normal. I eye him. "You were so mad at him," I say.

His brows pull together.

The others sense we're about to have a talk, so they leave us be. After watching them leave, I swallow and try to piece together what I'm feeling in my head. "I thought you were so pissed at him because he tackled you. He hurt you." I shake my head. "I didn't know you were as mad about the other thing."

Reid moves closer. "It wasn't just another thing," he says, mocking my words. "What they did to you was terrible."

"What they did to *you* was terrible. I got out of it okay. Nothing actually happened."

"Listen," Reid says, "the fact that they tried to do anything to you pisses me off. The fact that they tried to do that," he shakes his head, his throat working. "It makes me see red, Briar. No one does that to you." His hand moves down my body, cupping my bottom before moving up again. "It tears me up inside to know I wasn't the one who saved you from that."

I'd argue with him, but it wouldn't do any good.

"What they did to me was physical, but what they could've done to you was much worse. Do you think he would've just stopped at taking pictures? Do you think he couldn't have been talked into anything else? I wouldn't put anything past her, Briar." My face must fall because he turns my chin up so I can look into his face. "Nothing like that is going to happen to you while I'm around."

"I know," I say, my voice a whisper.

He leans down, sealing my lips to his. He feels so good that I deepen the kiss right here in Sasha's garage. He moans into my mouth, and his hands wander down to cup my ass before he easily plucks me from the ground, hoisting me up to his hips. I wrap my legs around him, bringing him closer until his erection makes me gasp free of his mouth.

"I can't get enough of you," he says.

My ass hits a solid surface, and I look around. I'm sitting on the Pontine family freezer, but I don't care. I pull Reid toward me again, reaching my hands under his shirt to feel his hard chest while our tongues war with one another.

"I don't have any resolve around you," he says, shuddering.

"I think you just like doing it in semi-public areas."

"As long as no one else gets to see you." His hand reaches between us, finding my clit through my flimsy leggings. I arch back, a silent cry on my lips. "Mmm," he murmurs. "I bet you're already wet, aren't you?"

I nod, reveling in the sensations his slight touch gives me. His hands move up to the tops of my leggings and tug down. I lift up, and he drags my bottoms and panties away in one pull. He yanks me forward until I'm almost teetering on the edge of the freezer, and then he pushes my knees apart, baring me to him.

"Reid," I say. My insides clench, and my heart is in my throat. The door to the house is still slightly ajar, and who knows if someone will come back looking for us to see if we're done talking. I doubt Reid is thinking about any of that though because he swoops down, his tongue on me before I can process the jolt that moves through me. "Oh God."

His tongue plays over my clit, licking and sucking. My nipples harden under my bra. "I'm so fucking hard. I'm going to make you come then slide inside you," he says, breathless.

He doesn't have to wait very long. His expert tongue, the fear of getting caught, his words, everything combined heightens my arousal until I'm panting and diving my hands into his hair, pulling him closer. "Oh God," I moan again, gasping when my orgasm hits hard and fast.

My muscles tighten and release as Reid steps back. He grabs a condom from his pocket and throws it next to me on the freezer while he unzips his jeans, tugging his pants down until his cock springs free.

A bead of cum glistens at the tip. I take the condom package and rip it open, pulling out the rubber inside. He helps me guide it on him, and I lean back, spreading my legs wide, beckoning him in. "God, you're so beautiful," he whispers.

He moves forward, guiding his cock to my entrance until he pushes inside, groaning when he's fully seated.

"And tight."

He moves inside me like it pains him. Each time he moves, he curses, then moves faster, harder. All I can do is hold on to him while he pumps in and out in short strokes that drive me higher and higher.

"God, I want to fuck you over and over again, Briar."

His assaults intensify until he hits a spot inside me that makes me want to crawl up a wall. It's pain and pleasure at the same time, and once he hits it, it only takes me a few more strokes to climax. As soon as mine hits, he follows me, the height of his excitement a short burst, but his aftershocks are slow and steady rocks into me until we're wrapped in one another's arms, breaths sawing in and out of us.

Finally, he kisses my neck. "We should get dressed. I need to take everyone home." He moans as he pulls out. "Maybe I'll sneak inside your room again tonight. I want to hold you."

He helps me pull my leggings back on and sees to it that he's dressed before he takes my hand, then runs his free hand through my hair, hopefully making it an appropriate amount of mussed up without making it look like we just had sex.

He leans over and kisses my cheek. "Don't worry about anything. I'll figure this out."

I want to give in to him, but I can't. He's more focused on making sure I'm okay when he really needs to be worrying about himself. And since he won't do it, I'll have to.

14

On Monday, Reid picks me up for school again. My parents seem to be getting used to the idea of us being a couple. Mom stops side-eyeing me whenever he's there, and she hasn't brought up the idea of shipping me off to her parents' house again either. Thankfully.

School goes by slow yet fast at the same time. I'm paying more attention than I was when my thoughts were wrapped around what happened to Brady. It almost feels like things are going back to normal since Brady's death. You know, if having a vindictive bitch after you and your boyfriend is normal. My grades are crawling back up, which I know my parents will like. Maybe that's the entire reason they haven't threatened to move me in with Grandma and Grandpa again. If that's the case, I'm going to keep at it.

When I get to English, Mr. Shaver tells me Oscar's waiting for me in the library to work on our project. Actually, it doesn't quite go down like that. When I walk into class, he looks at me like I'm losing it, asking me what I'm doing in class when Mr. Drego is in the library working on our project. He hands me a pass, dismisses me, and I walk to the library with a scowl on my face.

When I walk in, Oscar has the book out on one of the long tables in the back. He looks up as I approach. "There you are."

"You could've told me you got permission to meet in the library again, so I didn't look like an asshole."

A smile quirks his lips up. "It dawned on me that I didn't have your number to tell you."

"Ha." I look at him like he's crazy. "I don't think we need to be exchanging cell phone numbers."

"Why? Your boyfriend gets jealous?"

"Of your ass? Doubtful."

Oscar leans back in his chair, looking at me like he thinks this is a fun game. "Why did you come to Sasha's party Friday?"

"Why did you lie and tell her you invited us?"

He taps his pen against the wooden table between

us. "I like to see things play out. Plus," he looks around, checking the area for any prying ears. Though, why anyone would want to be listening in on us is a mystery to me. "I think it's funny when Sasha gets pissed."

"Some boyfriend."

"We're not dating," he says.

"Oh, right. Some fuck buddy."

He shrugs like he has no problem in the world being categorized like that. He doesn't, I imagine. He's a man of opportunity after all. I guess that rule applies to women too, not just situations that fall into his lap.

I set my bookbag down and sigh. It's pointless to try to argue with this kid. You can't argue with someone who has completely different morals than you. "I'm going to grab that literary text I was reading the other day," I tell him, referencing a book I found in the library that compares different classics. *The Great Gatsby* is one of them.

He goes back to reading the book, so I just meander through the stacks, heading into the non-fiction section that's even further back in the library than the table we're sitting at lies. The fiction is front and center in the library, an enticement to try to get more students to come in, I guess. But I usually only see the same people in here over and over again, except for people like Oscar who are researching a project. I head down between two stacks, scanning the multi-colored spines for the one I want at the far end. Finding it, I tip it out between two other books. When I go to grab it though, another hand is already there, blocking me.

I look up to find Oscar standing over me, his eyes leveled at my own. There's a different look in his eye than there was when we were out at the table. "Really," he whispers gruffly. "What were you doing at Sasha's party?"

I snatch the book out of his hand. "None of your business."

The wrinkles in between his eyes deepen as he narrows his gaze even more. His eyes are so dark it looks like I'm staring into a bottomless pit. My stomach churns. I quickly look behind him and realize it's just the two of us. It's quiet in the library anyway, but I can't even hear the hum of the copy machine or the librarian at the front desk shifting through her paperwork like before.

Oscar moves in closer. I try not to take a step back, but when he gets too close, I can't help myself. I move away, putting distance between us, trying to steady my beating heart. I know this guy hasn't done anything directly to me or the guys, but his "girlfriend" has. I don't trust him. Not by a long shot.

"You know what I think?"

"Enlighten me," I deadpan.

This makes his upper lip tip up in the corners and his eyes flare with interest. "I think you came for two reasons. One, to piss Sasha off. Congratulations, that worked." He leans against the bookcase, but tips his head back toward me like this is just a walk in the park for him. "What's annoying is she didn't fuck me that night because I told her I invited you guys."

I push out my lower lip and pout exaggeratedly. "That's terrible. I hope you'll survive."

He drags his gaze up and down me, making my skin buzz in response. It's like a warning bell, something telling me Oscar's not only an asshole, he could be something far creepier too. I try to push past him and go back to the table where there are more people around, but he grabs my arm, keeping me trapped in the stacks. "Now, that's not very nice. We're having a conversation here."

"We can have the same conversation out at the table," I tell him, looking past my shoulder to his still casual stance.

Oscar shakes his head. "I can't do that. Sasha likes to check up on me. Last time, one of her minions saw us in here working on our project, and she went ape shit. She really is jealous of you, Briar," he says, leering at me again. "Sure, she calls you names and tears you down, but that's just really her way of saying you're a threat. In her mind, she still can't understand how you got Reid away from her."

I sigh. "I try not to think about what that vapid bitch is thinking."

Oscar lets my wrist go and crosses his arms in front of his chest. "Me? I like to know my enemies."

"Your enemy?" My eyebrows shoot up. "Didn't she save you from Rawley Heights? Didn't she give you the starting quarterback position here? Sounds like she's your ally to me."

"You're naïve, Briar. It's adorable. I wish we all could be as innocent as you." He lifts his hand. I freeze when I notice he's going for my face. My heart shoots up into my throat, and I stare at his fingers getting closer and closer to my cheek, but I can't move. My heart thumps, thumps. His eyes track away, moving to mine instead of his intended target. Whatever he sees there stops him. He closes his fist and brings his hand back to his side. "I see why Reid wanted you over her. Sasha will never get it though. She'll never understand why man after man will pick someone like you over someone like her. Even when she finally settles down and gets the guy she deserves, he'll fuck someone like you on the side while she's stuck at home, staring at her kids while simultaneously watching the clock, wondering where life went wrong."

"That was...deep," I say. And a lot of trivial information.

"It's the truth."

I stare into his eyes, watching the shadows flicker there. I believe him. I know I shouldn't, but it feels like Oscar knows what he's talking about in this respect. He understands the seedier side of life. "You never said what the second reason was. Why we came to Sasha's party..."

He licks his lips and moves his stare to the threadbare carpet at our feet. The library is one of the few places in the building that has carpet. It's a built in sound barrier as are the stacks enclosing us in. "You want to take her down. You think finding something on her is going to do it." He lifts his hands. "I get it. If I were you, I'd want to take her out too. I think you need to think bigger than that though. Most of the students already know she took that picture of you. Hell, they're the ones calling you Tiny Tits. Do you think that will change if they find out she got in trouble for it? That she was fined and has to do community service?" He shakes his head. "No, it won't, Briar. You're still going to be Tiny Tits, and she's still going to be a bitch. No one's arguing that fact. She's hated. So, what? Do something more." He drops his gaze to my chest pointedly. "For the record, I'd never call you Tiny Tits. I think they're a nice size. The shape is on point, too."

I shiver. His look makes me want to put on several layers of clothes.

His mouth quirks up. "Sorry. I usually say what I mean. I'm not used to sweet girls like you getting offended."

"Are you telling me that's a line to some girls?"

"Works like a charm."

I can see how that would work for him. Back in Rawley Heights, Oscar was Reid. If Reid said that to a girl, he could probably get that girl to sleep with him too. The difference is, Reid would never do that. No, he's not a saint. He's just not a pig like Oscar.

"You're pretty judgey for someone who wants to take someone else down, you know that? Love thy neighbor and all that shit. You're just as bad as me. You just don't know it yet."

His words make my stomach upheave, like the world is shifting underneath us. My cell vibrates. Oscar keeps the confident smirk on his face while I take it out and check it. A shadow falls over the text I just got from Lex, and I look up to see Oscar reading the screen at the same time I do.

"When are you going to cut that poor guy loose?"

"What?"

"Lex," he says. "He's clearly in love with you, and he hasn't gotten the memo yet that you're never going to be with him." His lips pull up. "You're just like any other girl. You want the bad boy, but keep the other on the side burner to play with."

"Fuck you," I growl.

Oscar's face radiates excitement. He's clearly enjoying all of this, but it's making my stomach turn. I already know how Lex feels about me. I've seen the looks Reid's given him lately, too. In my heart of hearts, I know it's only a matter of time before this all blows up in my face. "Cut him loose," Oscar says. "It's the right thing to do."

My mouth opens. A million things come to mind to snap back at him with, but none of them eke past my lips. I turn quickly, my hair spiraling out around me, and I stomp back to the table just as the bell rings overhead. I curse under my breath and shove the book I have in my hands back on a re-shelve cart before heading for my bookbag. Behind me, Oscar starts to say something, but Lex opens the library door. He scans the crowd and then makes his way over to me. His face is filled with hard lines. Stress. The only thing that lights when he sees me are his eyes.

Guilt twists my stomach. *I shouldn't have done what I did with him*, I think again.. It was wrong.

"Hey," he says, his gaze shifting beyond me. His glare intensifies, so I can only guess he's spotted Oscar following me out of the back of the library. "Everything good?" he asks, still watching the figure behind me.

"I can handle Oscar," I say, probably with a little more bite than I mean to.

This makes Lex switch his gaze to me. My heart pumps inside, watching the worry lines etch onto his face.

"What's up, Jones?" Oscar asks, grabbing his copy of *The Great Gatsby* and throwing it into his bookbag before hiking it onto his shoulder.

Lex grunts in response, but then says, "Drego," with a nod. I watch as they evaluate one another, Oscar's words thrumming in my ears. *Cut him loose. It's the right thing to do.*

I'm not holding him here, I counter, speaking up against that tiny voice inside my head. *I swear. He knows Reid and I are together. He knows.*

Oscar gives me a knowing look as Lex won't take his eyes off me. It curdles my stomach so much that my hand comes to rest there, like it's trying to hold everything in place.

I'm not doing that to Lex, am I?

15

*R*eid and I walk out of school together, hand-in-hand. He's been looking at me weird all day. It's probably the unnerved feeling I have inside coming out on the outside, but I don't know how to explain to him what's going on in my head. So, every time he asks what's wrong, I tell him nothing. I just shrug, smile a false smile for him, and tell him I'm good. He can see through all of it. He saw through all the Brady bullshit before, so when a car horn beeps as we walk out, and my mom lowers the window to wave at us, I feel him tighten up.

I think I may have just dodged a car ride filled with him pestering me with questions about what's bothering me. Not that I don't want to talk to him about what Oscar said, but I also don't want him to get upset.

I don't want him to hate Lex or fight with him or anything else he'll think about doing.

He's the one who has to steer me toward the car. She smiles at him. "Hi, Reid. I've got to steal Briar away."

He places his hand on the door, staring inside while his hand tightens around mine. "No problem, Mrs. Page. Do you mind if I come over after practice?"

She nods. "That should be fine. I'll set an extra plate for you."

Reid squeezes my hand tight, then leans over to kiss my temple. "See you soon," he breathes, and I wonder if my mom can notice how he affects me with just that barest of touches.

He opens the car door for me, and I slide inside. Mom gives him a wave and then pulls around to the line of cars waiting to get out of the parking lot. I set my bag down between my legs and pull the seatbelt over, locking it in place. "What's up?" I ask.

She takes a deep breath and lets it out in a huff. "I had a talk with Mrs. Parker today…"

Like I needed to feel more sick. "Oh yeah?"

She pulls out of the parking lot, pushing down on the accelerator and throwing me back in the seat. Mom sneaks a peek over at me. "I know why you didn't say anything to me, but I wish you had. I wish I hadn't heard from your boyfriend's mom that you're sexually active."

My stomach revolts. "I'm—"

"You're not in trouble," she says, clarifying. "I totally get it. I didn't give Brady a hard time when I found out about him and Jules, and I'm not going to be the parent who worries more about her daughter than her son. I just wish you'd told me," she says.

I can feel my face flush. Honestly, I'd rather be a bunch of different places than here right now. "I didn't want to worry you about one more thing, and..." I hesitate before I say the next thing. "We haven't been on the best of terms lately either. I didn't want to give you another reason to get disappointed in me."

Mom sighs again. "Oh, Briar." Those two words sound like disappointment wrapped into a big, black bow. I almost tune her out. Almost. "I know," she says. "I get it. We need to both do better, starting now. You can stop looking at me like I'm about to ship you off to a different state at any moment, and I can start treating you like you're back at square one. Okay?"

"Okay..." I say, a little hesitantly.

"Have you guys been careful so far?" Mom asks. "I assume so. I know Reid's not a virgin, and I'm sure the Parkers have already drilled that into him."

"Yes, we've been careful," I tell her.

She nods, and I see a little of the small lines smooth out over her face. "That's good. I got an appointment for you at the OBGYN. We're going to get you on birth control. That doesn't mean you should stop using condoms. I'd prefer it if you use condoms," she tacks on. "You can't be too careful. You and Reid have everything going for you guys. I've been checking the school portal, so I know how much your grades have improved, Briar. I'm...proud of you. Really proud of you. I know how much our lives were turned upside down after what happened to Brady. I don't like the way you handled some things, but that doesn't mean I don't understand it. Okay? We'll never forget Brady, but hopefully we can get back to a new normal."

I don't know what it is, but whenever my mom talks about Brady, grief grips me. It squeezes my heart until it's too painful. Staring at other people's sadness is sometimes worse than feeling your own. My eyes burn, and I clear my throat, doing everything I can to stop reacting this way.

Mom reaches over and puts her hand on my thigh, giving me a quick squeeze. "I know," she says. "I know."

I take a few minutes to gather myself and then I look over at Mom. "You're not mad that Reid and I are having sex? You're not going to yell at him, are you?"

Mom laughs, the sound genuine. Maybe even one of the first genuine laughs I've heard since Brady died. "No, I'm not going to yell at him. Your father might want to have a talk with him, but you're not going to hear anything from me. I don't know if I told you before how your grandmother handled my first time talk, but it wasn't pretty. I swore I would never do that to my kids. I understand you're going to have sex. And you love Reid..." She looks over at me like she's trying to gauge how much I really do love him. I smile at her even though my ears are probably pink from what she said sex two seconds earlier. "He loves you too. Mrs. Parker also loves you," she says. "You should've heard her go on and on about how much she misses you."

Her face falls, and I see her chew her bottom lip. "I didn't tell her about Reid and me," I say. "Reid didn't either. She kind of walked in on us."

"Oh God," Mom says, horrified.

"No, not that," I say immediately. "It was in the morning. I was in his bed. She put two and two together."

Mom clutches her chest. She calms down after a moment. "I probably wouldn't have sent you there while Dad and I took our vacation if we'd known you were dating."

Busted.

"Sorry," I tell her. "It kind of just happened."

She takes a left into a single story cement building. An hour and about a dozen cringe-worthy moments later, I walk out with birth control pills and am told I can start taking them tomorrow. My mom seems satisfied, and I imagine she is. I don't want to get pregnant either. I have things I want to do, and a baby doesn't factor into them. Even if the appointment was embarrassing, I'd rather be thinking about all of this than not and wind up turning my whole life upside down just because I didn't want to worry about something being embarrassing. I look over at her as she drives us home. "Thanks for this, Mom. And for being cool about Reid and me."

Her fingers tense on the steering wheel. "You know I love Reid," she says. "But that doesn't mean I want to walk in on you guys, you understand?"

Wow. She's really stuck on that. "Yeah, Mom. We don't want that either."

A small laugh trickles out of her, which turns into a huge laugh. It keeps coming out of her like she's had it held in for a while. She wipes tears away from her eyes, and I totally get it. Emotions are fucked up. Sad one moment, happy the next. You can be crying when you're sad and crying when you're happy. One thing leads to another and you may have started out happy, but ended up sad.

I reach over and pat her arm. "I'm sure Brady handled this much better."

Mom laughs again. "Actually, I think he was way more embarrassed than you."

I take that memory my mom's reliving in her mind and let it go, giving her this moment. Maybe some other day I'll ask her how it went when she found out Brady was having sex with Jules, but not right now. Right now, I'm going to let her have it to herself.

I lean back in the seat, closing my eyes for a moment, pushing aside thoughts on what Brady might think of Reid and I having sex and just hold on to the tiny paper bag in my hand that's just more evidence of how my world is changing without Brady in it.

When Mom and I pull in and go into the house, Reid's already there. I can tell from the look on his face that my dad probably already had a talk with him. I cringe inwardly, but I'm also relieved I didn't have to be there for that one. We eat dinner together, and then Reid and I retreat to my room to do homework, which my mom—again—says to keep the door open. We do, but that doesn't mean we don't sneak kisses. And that also doesn't mean I can't avoid the questions from earlier that I know Reid was burning to ask.

I'm lying on my stomach, a book open in front of me. Reid has my desk chair pulled to the side of the bed. He's hunched over his own book, but he's too busy dragging his fingers up and down my side to pay attention to what he's reading. Well, at least, I'm too preoccupied with what he's doing that I've had to read the same page five times because it hasn't sunk in once. "You know," he says, his voice low. When he pitches it like that, it does twisty things to my insides. "You can't avoid my questions forever. Even if your dad did try to talk to me about sex."

I look up, eyes round, but then I laugh into the comforter, using the thick fabric to stifle the sound. "How'd that go, by the way?"

"We'll talk about you making it up to me later." His eyes glint with amusement, but his face turns serious soon afterward. "I know something happened today, Briar. Lex tells me you and Oscar were working together in the library. Is it about him? Did he say something to you?"

"He says a lot of things," I confess, rolling my eyes. "That boy really loves to hear himself talk."

"Stop avoiding the question."

I turn over on my stomach, looking up at him. He moves around and leans over the bed. I prop myself up, so we're staring at each other face-to-face. "He knows we want to get back at Sasha."

His jaw tightens. "Did he threaten you?"

I shake my head. "He seems almost like he wants to help," I say, grudgingly.

"Oscar Drego is not our friend."

"I agree," I tell him. "One-hundred percent."

Reid relaxes a little. "So, that's it?"

I tuck my bottom lip between my teeth. I don't know how to bring Lex up without pissing Reid off. Reid's jealous, and I'm not even sure he'll even give Lex a break.

"You can tell me," Reid says. His hand reaches out to trace the line of my jaw.

I swallow. "It's Lex," I say finally. "Oscar told me I needed to cut him loose. That he can tell how much Lex… likes me," I say, my tongue feeling too large for my mouth as I stumble over the word like. That wasn't exactly what Oscar said, but I'm not going to use the L word. "He made it seem like I was being mean to him, but I don't—."

Reid sighs. He gets up from the chair and starts to pace the room. His fingers dive into his hair until it looks like he's going to tear it out by the roots. I sit up, forcing my legs over the bed to watch him. "It's not you," Reid says. "Oscar's wrong about that. It's not you at all. I was kind of hoping he'd get over it after he saw you and I together, but it doesn't seem to be working that way. He's been pissing me off lately. Always watching you, using excuses to touch you."

"Reid," I say. When he looks over at me, I don't know what to say. I don't want them to fight. I can't stand the tension that's filling the room right now. For as long as I've known these guys, it's always been the four of them. Now, after Brady's death, it's only three. Something else can't happen to these guys. Not fighting over me. That's so...dumb.

"I think I'm going to have a talk with him again."

"Is that really necessary?" I ask, biting my lip.

"Briar, nothing's going to change the way I feel about Lex, but Oscar's right. It's not fair to him if we don't shut this shit down."

"Does that mean I should talk to him?"

A growl escapes Reid lips, but then he looks guilty. "If I was a better man, I'd probably just let him have you. He's better than me."

"Don't say that," I say, standing. "This is just a fucked up situation that I started. If I hadn't—" I cut myself off when Reid throws a look at me. "If I hadn't done what I did, maybe Lex wouldn't, you know, like me like he does."

Reid shakes his head. "It's not that. Lex can separate sex and feelings, trust me. It's just you, Briar."

I hold my head in my hands. Reid comes over, leans down to kiss me on the top of the head, and then packs up his book bag. "Leaving?"

"I might as well get this over with."

"Be nice to him," I say.

Reid stills, shooting me a look. I hold his gaze, not backing down. I know the situation is all twisted, but it's Lex and Reid. I'm not coming between them. Never. I couldn't.

"I'll see you tomorrow," he says, as he strides out the open bedroom door. I hear him say good night to my parents and then the front door closes. My stomach twists as his car starts, and I hear it pull down the driveway.

It feels like something's about to change. For good. And I don't like it.

16

I don't hear from Reid the rest of the night, but in the morning, he sends me a single text. **Cade's picking you up.**

I really want my own car. I hate the fact that they're driving my ass around everywhere. It's one thing when it's Reid because I know he wants to, but Cade's a different story. I feel like I'm putting him out.

The bagel I made for him is hot in my hand when I hear him beep outside. I tell my parents I'll see them after school and walk outside. "Sorry," I tell him, as soon as I open the door. I shove the bagel in his face.

He chuckles. "No problem, Shortie."

"So, where's Reid?" I ask. I'm digging for information, yes. I'm not ashamed to admit it. Reid doesn't send the most forthcoming texts, loaded with information that sets me at ease. They're actually the exact opposite.

"Up late fighting with Lex. He overslept."

My stomach squeezes. I look over at Cade. He takes a huge bite out of the bagel and shrugs, acting like nothing's wrong. I look away, feeling like this is all my fault.

"You want my advice?" Cade asks.

"Not really."

He laughs. "Too bad. Listen, Briar, those two are so alike it's crazy. They need to blow off steam, let them."

"Do you know what they're fighting about?"

He gives me a pointed look. "I'm not an idiot."

"Yeah, well, what am I supposed to do about it?"

"You made your choice, right? It seems to me there's not anything you can do about it. Lex just needs to move on or not. It's his decision."

"Why do you sound so blasé about it? They're your friends."

He shrugs. "Because I can't imagine Lex not moving on. That's why. And listen, they're probably going to go all caveman on you, so if you need someone to hang around with who isn't thinking about fucking you, give me a call."

He winks, and I sigh, dropping my head to the window, so I can look outside.

"Okay, maybe I've thought about fucking you a couple of times. You don't have to act so sad about it," he finally says.

I peer over my shoulder to give him a dirty look, but the look on his face makes me laugh. "I really hate you sometimes."

"You love me."

I turn to look out the window again. "Except the times I hate you."

Cade's chuckle is deep and throaty. He polishes off the bagel and wipes his hands on his jeans. "Hey, you think Jules is doing okay lately?"

I sag into the car door and turn toward him. His face is thoughtful. "Yeah, I do," I tell him. "How are you doing?"

He blinks. He takes a while to respond, and I realize I've probably never asked Cade that question regarding Brady. He leans back in his seat, leaving one hand on the steering wheel while the other touches his chin thoughtfully. "I'm doing okay, Briar." He looks over to give me a small smile and reaches out to pat my leg. "I'm glad your goth phase is over."

I shake my head and laugh. "You just can't stand to have things be serious for a minute, can you?"

His lips turn up even higher. "Nah. Not my style. You know I loved your brother, though, right?"

I grasp his hand in mine and squeeze once. "I know, Farmer."

He sighs and our hands slip out of one another's naturally. I envy Cade a little. I wish I could find something to smile about every day. Maybe it would ease my soul. To him, at least on the outside, it seems like he thinks everything's always going to work out.

"Hmm," Cade says thoughtfully.

He pulls me into the present as he swings into the school parking lot. There are a few cars lined up in front of the main glass doors. The cars are old, busted up. Some of them have several parts from different cars. One has a car door that's a different color than the rest of the vehicle. The other has a blue hood with a white body. Big, tough looking guys are standing out in front of the cars, their arms crossed over their chests. They look pretty pissed. "What's this about?"

When Cade pulls into a parking space, we have a front-row seat of Oscar walking toward them. All the newcomers stiffen and stand to their full heights. "Well, shit," Cade says.

"What is it?"

"If I'm not mistaken, that's the O line at Rawley Heights."

"The O line? Oscar's O line."

"Not anymore," Cade says, sighing. He pushes the

car door open and gets out. It slams behind him, and I immediately fumble out of the car, hot on his heels. "Stay back," he barks over his shoulder at me, but my feet don't stop.

Up ahead, I hear Oscar say, "Hey, guys," in his normal, shit-eating grin tone. "Didn't think I'd catch you guys way the hell out here. What's up?"

The guy in the middle shakes out his hands and approaches Oscar. He's got a much wider girth than his old teammate, taller too. It looks like the guy could flick out his pinkie and send him flying. "Drego, nice digs," the guy says, looking appreciatively back over his shoulder at the school. "Got yourself set up pretty nice here, huh? I hear your mom's nice and comfortable, too."

Oscar shrugs. "You know, living the dream."

Cade and I approach Oscar. From my peripheral, I see a few other of our football players lurking near the sides. I'd feel a lot safer if Lex were around. I'd usually say Reid, but he can't be involved in any sort of fight right now with his head injury, so he's not an option.

As cool as can be, Cade greets the visitors and then slings his arm around Oscar. "Dude, you didn't tell me your old pals were swinging by the school."

"I wasn't aware," Oscar says. His body is tight,

bunched up. He looks like he could spring at any moment.

The lead guy shifts, and a glint of reflecting light shines into my eyes from his midsection before he pulls his coat back together. My heart stops for a second. I've seen enough movies to know that was a gun. Holy fuck. These dudes from Rawley Heights are no joke.

Behind them, a car door swings open, and a guy gets out. Using a golf club as a cane, he saddles up to the head guy who's staring at Oscar like he wants to kick his ass and drag his face over rough pavement.

To our right, I see a flash of blonde move past. I look up when Oscar does and see Sasha moving around the cars. Sparing a glance back, she sees Oscar, but keeps moving around the cars to head into school. "Dirty bitch," I mumble. This is all her fault. She brought Oscar here, and now his old teammates look pretty put out by that fact.

Oscar turns toward me after my words reach his ears. He sees me there, and his eyes widen.

I smile at him, then take that opportunity to talk. "Hey, aren't we supposed to work on our project this morning? If we get a bad grade because of you, I'm going to be pissed."

"And you are?" the guy with the golf club asks.

"Briar Page," I tell him. I don't know why I use

my last name, maybe hoping these guys will recognize it and leave me out of it. But for some reason, I'm trying to help Oscar. Or maybe it's just because Cade came this way, and I'm helping Cade. That must be what it is. I wouldn't let him come over here by myself.

The guy looks me up and down and dismisses me, returning his stare to Oscar. "Stuck up school bitches, preppy football player friends. It's like we don't even know you, Drego."

Oscar scoffs. "Please. You guys know me."

He's trying to act hard, and I don't know, maybe it's coming across like that. But to me, I see the fear behind it, and I can't believe Sasha just left him to his own devices. She clearly noticed something was going down. Who the hell knows what she thinks? The two deserve each other, I guess.

I grab Cade's arm as the one guy starts to tap his golf club against the pavement. Suddenly, a big body moves in front of me. I recognize Lex's back, looking every bit as dangerous as the guys in front of us. His voice comes out smooth with a hint of anger. "What's going on Oscar?"

Oscar gestures towards the guys across from us. With Lex making an appearance, other Spring Hill football players move in, making my shoulders relax some. "These are my old teammates. I think they wanted to come see what I was up to here."

"Heard you won your last game," the big guy in the middle says.

"We did," Oscar says.

A few of the other football players nod in agreement. I can't help but think that if this is the place Oscar came from, maybe I should be more scared of him than I am. These guys clearly came here to play dirty. Are they pissed he left them to come play for us?

"How nice," the guy sneers. "Maybe you'll win the All-State like you always wanted."

Oscar shrugs. "If I'm lucky."

Another figure comes in tight. He puts his arm around me, and instead of calming me down, I freeze. It's Reid, so I should feel safer, but I can't help but think if he gets hit with that golf club, he's done for. He might not wake up this time, just like Brady.

The Rawley Heights guys look up, assessing Reid and I standing there. Reid kisses my temple and goes to lead me away, but a guy on the end speaks up. "You must hate Oscar as much as we do," he says.

"I'm not his biggest fan if that's what you mean," Reid says, earning some guffaws from the crowd.

The guy quirks a devilish smile and looks at Oscar. "When Parker returns to *his* team, don't think you're going to head back to Rawley to play, motherfucker. You're done."

The guy with the golf club brings it up. I freeze for a moment, wondering what the hell's about to happen, but all he does is swing it up on his shoulder like he just teed up from the first hole. The other Rawley guys, too, start to put away different weapons I didn't even realize they had. There's the guy with the gun who leans back against the car. A few guys I see stick things back in their pockets, so who the hell knows what they had? All I'm getting from this is that I'm not equipped to deal with these kinds of fights.

Our principal walks out, assessing the situation with a cursory glance. He puts his hands on his hips. "Spring Hill students, get inside." Coach Jackson comes out next along with Ms. Lyons. "Your education awaits. If you're from another school, I think you also have somewhere else to be."

The crowd starts to disperse. Reid moves me away first, but I keep checking back over my shoulder. Cade leaves a moment before Oscar does, and Oscar and his old teammates are the last to leave the staring contest. When we walk in through the doors, a breath releases. "What the hell just happened?" I gasp.

"Why were you out there?" Reid asks, turning me around to stare at me, his hands on my upper shoulders. He checks me over, looking up and down, an inspection that makes me shiver.

"Cade went up to them. I wasn't going to leave him alone."

Cade and Oscar walk in at that moment. Cade's not even walking with him though. He's walking in front of him while Oscar's jaw is set.

"Hey, you okay?" a voice asks me.

I look up to find Lex and gasp when I see his black eye.

He looks away sheepishly.

"Um, thanks for that," a voice says behind us. Cade, Lex, and Reid all turn, staring Oscar down. "I didn't know they were going to show up like that."

"Don't bring shit like that to my school," Reid says.

Oscar looks at me. I'm pinned between Lex and Reid, which he seems to notice right away. He acknowledges Lex's black eye and looks at me again, a quirk on his lips. "I'll make sure to tell them you don't want their gang-banging asses on your school property."

Reid moves fast. He takes Oscar by surprise, holding him up against a locker. "If my girl gets hurt because of you, we'll be fighting about more than fucking football, asshole. You understand?"

Oscar pushes him off and rearranges the collar of

his shirt. "I understand, Big Man." He looks at me and then walks away, casually walking down the hall like he owns the place. Sasha has no idea what she fucking did, does she? And she doesn't care if everyone else fights as long as she gets what she wanted in the first place...to take Reid down and to humiliate me. All because Reid didn't want her anymore. Her pettiness is unreal.

But that's not the only thing I have to worry about right now. I turn toward Lex, who's keeping his black eye away from me. I glare at Reid, but he just stares back at me. "What happened?"

"Oh shit," Cade says. Jules walks up at that moment, completely oblivious to what's going on. Cade takes her arm and leads her away. "Come on, Jules. We need to be anywhere but here."

I watch them go, flinging Cade a dirty look. Coward. But it's Reid's voice that breaks through. "Lex and I had a discussion last night. That's all."

"This is stupid," I say, pleading with him. "Did you hit Lex?"

"It's fine," Lex says.

Reid all but growls. "I did. Because the dumbass doesn't know when to give up, and I'd do it again. For you, I'd do anything, Briar."

I just stare at him, mouth slightly open. This wasn't

what I wanted at all. Why couldn't they just talk? "I don't want you guys to fight."

"Too late," Reid says.

Lex is staying quiet. There are two pink circles on his cheeks like he's embarrassed, which pains me. I want to comfort Lex and scream at Reid, but at the same time, I don't want to be caught in the middle. Instead, I just shake my head and walk away.

"Where are you going?" Reid asks, his voice strained.

"Somewhere. Anywhere," I say, frustration settling in. "As long as it's not near you."

Guilt slams into me the moment those words leave my mouth, but I run away from it. From all of it. Maybe this was why Brady didn't think it was a good idea to get involved with Reid. Did he foresee all this? Did he know what was going to happen before it even did?

All I know is, I want my cake and eat it too. I want Reid by my side, and I want Lex to be okay with it. But that's a perfect world, and if anyone should know that this isn't a perfect world, it's me.

17

I meet Oscar in the library during English class again. We don't talk much until the bell rings for lunch, and I stay right where I am. He peers over at me, lines wrinkling his forehead. "Not going to lunch?"

I shrug. "I'm not hungry."

"Sounds like bullshit to me," Oscar says. He seems tired, or more like he has a hundred different things on his mind. "Sounds more like you want to avoid the fact that your boyfriend punched his best friend because they're both in love with you."

I really fucking hate that he knows so much. I also hate the fact that I don't have anyone else to talk to but Jules. It makes me want to tell Oscar everything, all the pent up frustration I'm feeling because of it, but it's only because he's right here and I haven't been able to think about anything else all day but Lex's black eye and what it symbolizes.

Instead of saying all that, I look up. "Something like that."

"I admit, I didn't think Reid was going to take it that far."

My tongue itches to move. My lips ache to open, to agree with him, but I hold it back. "Nice ex friends you got there from Rawley Heights," I say instead.

"Ha," he says, emotionless.

"Did you know they were going to be that pissed?"

"To come at me at my new school?" He moves his head back and forth like he's weighing the two sides. "Yeah, I did."

I give him a disbelieving look. "Then why the fuck would you do it? And I don't know if you noticed, but Sasha couldn't get far enough away fast enough. She doesn't give a shit about you."

"And you do?" he asks. "Because you were there."

"I was there for Cade."

Oscar's gaze lowers. "I knew what I was getting into when I agreed to do it. Sasha and I have an understanding. I'm not her knight in shining armor, and she's no fucking princess. But we have a few things in common."

"Why do I think the things you have in common are probably also the worst traits about you?"

"So, you have been paying attention?"

I shake my head, wondering why the hell I even engage in conversation with him. He brought those thugs to our school. Some terrible shit could've happened to my friends because of it. But no matter how much I want to blame it all on Oscar, I can't. Sasha's the reason why Oscar is even here.

"Listen, I won't forget what you and your friends did for me out there. If they weren't around, they probably would've busted my head in."

"Yeah, I saw the golf club. And was that a gun?" I ask, almost incredulously.

"Rawley Heights isn't a very nice area. You think you got it bad. Not even fucking close."

I slice a look toward him. He seems to know an awful lot about me. Or maybe that's just his way of trying to get me to say more. I don't engage him on that, but I do ask, "So, shit like that is a regular occurrence at Rawley Heights?"

"Metal detectors, police, fucked up teachers. Any sad story you've ever read about at a high school, Rawley Heights has. Why do you think I wanted to get the fuck out of there? The scouts don't even want to come to our games because it's so fucked up."

My heart pings. I hate that the more Oscar talks, the more I can see why he's done certain things. But, I hate the idea that he does things without caring who it affects. I'll never be able to get over that. "That's...terrible."

"It is what it is when you live in the projects. Everything's about the honor of having no honor. They work with their own set of rules, and I broke one. No one gets out of Rawley Heights. And if you do, they make you pay."

I lean back in my chair. "So, I take it that's not the last you'll be seeing of those guys?"

Oscar shakes his head. "Not by a long shot."

I exhale a breath, looking into Oscar's eyes. It's hard to think of him as the enemy's sidekick when there's a hint of fear underneath the surface. It makes him more human, and that I don't like. I want Reid to get better. I want him to take his spot back and leave Oscar in his wake. But I think that's what Oscar expects to happen to a poor guy from Rawley Heights. "She didn't save you, you know? Sasha."

Oscar bursts out laughing. "You think I think that?" He shakes his head. "I love how fucking innocent you are." He laughs for a few more seconds, then says, "Listen, I know she didn't save me. I know she has her own agenda. I said it before, and I'll keep saying it.

I'm a man of opportunity. I have to be. I saw a way out, and I fucking took it."

"Knowing the risks?"

"Knowing the risks, but also knowing I'm fucking scrappy when it comes to it. Right now, my mom's safe in a nice little townhouse. If I can keep this position, I'll be well on my way to college, away from the Heights, away from Spring Hill."

"Reid's not going to let you take his spot on the team, Oscar. You picked the wrong guy to stay down."

Oscar lifts his shoulders, a flash of darkness skating through his eyes. My body turns cold. Oscar would probably do anything he could to get what he wants, just like he said.

"Just remember you owe us for today," I tell him, throwing that in his face again. The last thing I want is for him to think he can really take Reid out of the picture by showing up with his own golf club.

He nods once, and I stand, throwing shit into my bookbag. I'm so caught up in what I'm doing I don't realize Oscar has left until a hand comes to rest on my shoulder. I flinch. My eyes move upward, and I see the empty chair Oscar had just been in.

"Sorry. I didn't mean to scare you."

It's Reid. I want so badly to just let him hold me, but what he did was wrong, so I don't say anything.

After a while, Reid sighs. "Listen, I know you're pissed at me, but that doesn't mean you should skip lunch." I finally look up at him. He's holding a bag of chips and an apple and shrugging. "It's all I could score from the line."

"Why did you do it?" I whisper, ignoring his sweet gesture. "Why did you hit Lex?"

"We had a disagreement."

"About?"

"You know what about, Briar."

"I won't come between you guys. I won't," I say again, my voice rising.

Reid looks around, then takes my bag and pulls me into the back of the library between the same two stacks Oscar and I had our lovely chat in. He places his hands on my upper shoulders. "You're right. You won't."

"You hit him."

"It's not the first time, and I'm sure it won't be the last. I only feel bad that he won't hit me back."

"Of course he won't," I say through clenched teeth. "You have a brain injury, Reid. Why would he risk that?"

Reid presses his lips together. "Just let Lex and I work it out."

I cross my arms over my chest. "If your way of

working things out is punching each other, I don't agree."

He lowers his gaze to the floor but squeezes my shoulders. After a while, he looks up again. His green eyes swirl with emotion. "Can I help it that I want to fight when it feels like someone wants to take the best thing I've ever had away from me? And the sooner Lex gets it, the better. The only thing that will make me stop fighting for you is if you tell me to stop. And I hope you don't ever do that." He sighs, pulling me to him. "That's what Lex and I talked about. I told him to lay off unless you asked him not to, and I told him I'd do the same. I told him that if you ever ask me to lay off, I'd do it in a heartbeat."

I hold on to him tighter at his words. I don't want to let him go, and I certainly don't want him to lay off. "Why does Lex have a black eye?"

"It took us a while to get to that point."

My shoulders sag, but Reid holds me tighter. The steady thump of his heartbeat calms me down, eventually. "So, everything's good now? Are you still fighting? I just want everything to go back to the way it was."

Reid moves me away at arm's length. He lifts his big hand to my cheek. "We're past that point, Briar. Don't get me wrong, I know how Lex is feeling. If you ever told me to stop, I'd..." His throat works. "I'd act the same as him. I told him I got it. But I also asked him for the sake of our friendship if he'd try to get past it. If he'd try to move on. That's one thing I can say for him. He might just love you as much as I do." His gaze hardens. "I hate to fucking admit that, but..." He shrugs, leaving the sentence unsaid. Leaving his thoughts unexplained.

I don't know what to do with that admission, so I just keep it inside me, locking it away in case I ever want to revisit this moment. Right now, though, I hope what Reid is saying is true. Hopefully the rest of us can go back to some place where it's okay for me to be in love with Reid and not with Lex, and no one cares.

"Please don't be mad at me."

I turn away and shake my head. "It's fine. I think." He gives me a look, pleading me with his eyes. "It's fine," I say, trying again. Mostly I'm just trying to mean it.

Reid lets out a breath of relief. "Good. So," He throws his arm around me. "I was thinking that since your mom and dad are cool with us being together now, maybe they can lift your punishment. My parents were wondering if you could come to dinner tonight."

I bite my lip. Mom and I did say we'd try to start back on square one. "I guess we can ask."

"I'll ask," he says. "She probably still likes me better."

I elbow him in the stomach. "Not so fast, Seven. We had a breakthrough talking about sex yesterday." I pull out my phone and type out a message to my mom, asking if I can go to Reid's house for dinner.

"Brave," Reid says. "Speaking of..." He trails off while leading me back to rest against a bookshelf. "You and I need to talk about you walking into a gang fight."

"They weren't fighting," I protest.

He leans over, his hot breath hitting my ear. "Not yet."

I squirm, feeling his breath coat my neck in tingling anticipation. It threads through my body, settling in my core until white hot heat burns there.

"That was naughty, Briar. Very naughty."

"I'm sorry?" I say, trying to sound convincing. Those guys would do the same for each other. It just felt natural.

He takes my hands and pins them above my head. "That didn't sound contrite enough." His green eyes spark with mischief.

My body buzzes, and I feel my nipples harden under my shirt. My chest heaves out between us, brushing against his own.

He leans over, kissing a path from my earlobe

down to my neck. My head falls back until the movement slides books out of the way. I lean against the shelving unit for support while Reid continues to place soft kisses on my skin. "I'm glad you wanted to be there for Cade, but next time, text all of us and head the other way. If something happened to you..." A shiver takes over his body, and he pulls away. "Okay?"

I nod, and his body leaves mine, leaving me flushed and cold at the same time in the absence of him.

I scowl, and he smirks. "Later," he promises. "If your mom says you can come over."

New goal: Convince Mom to let me go Reid's house.

18

*R*eid helps me out of his car after football practice. Mom sent a reluctant text right before school ended that said I could go to dinner and come right back home. When I walk inside Reid's house, I'm assaulted by memories of the first night I came home. How worried everyone was. How lost Reid looked. But the overall excitement I felt to seeing him alive, to seeing him mostly uninjured. I reach up on my tiptoes to kiss him, and he beams back at me. "What was that for?"

"Just because."

"You two are the cutest," I hear from down the hall which makes me smile. Mrs. Parker comes out from around the corner. "I'm so happy Pam decided to let you come over. I told her I'd watch over you, make sure you didn't sneak off to have sex."

My face blooms red, and Reid just blinks at his mother like he can't believe she just said that.

"Well, I had to promise her something," Mrs. Parker says. She starts off down the hallway. "Your dad's going to be a little late. He's with a client in Germantown. He said we could start without him."

I used to think it was odd that Reid's family ate so much earlier than other people, but I've been explained their diet schedule before. They actually eat six meals a day instead of the usual three. It helps keeps the metabolism going, I guess. So, they eat now and have a snack later. They also eat nothing past seven pm.

Reid doesn't stick to it all the time. It's kind of hard for him, considering he's at school, but there are always healthy snacks around the Parker house.

During dinner, Mrs. Parker talks to us about school and to Reid about his next doctor's appointment. We're close to finishing when Mr. Parker comes home, but we all sit around talking for a little while longer until Reid tells his parents we're going to do homework in his room. His mom releases us from the table, and we head upstairs without bookbags in our hands. Mine is still in his car, actually. "Homework?" I ask.

His lips tease up. "I love my mom," he says.

"I think *I* love your mom."

Reid walks me into the room and shuts the door behind us. It's easier getting away from parents at his house than it is at mine. We live in a ranch-style house, so all the bedrooms are on the same floor. Here, we can move upstairs, and his parents probably won't even bother us.

"Do you think your mom will realize she let us come up here unsupervised?"

"I'm counting on the fact that she doesn't. They're probably already talking about work."

Reid moves closer, taking my hands in his and moving me back against his bedroom door. He moves me into the same position he had me in the library earlier. My hands above my head, our bodies pressed close together. My mouth dries, and I blurt out. "I'm on birth control now. Mom made me get it, but the doctor says we shouldn't have unprotected sex for a while."

Reid blinks down at me, a small smile tugging at his lips. "You're too cute."

"I just didn't want you to think that you could go in, you know—"

"Bareback?" he asks.

Just the sound of that makes me groan. Our bodies

touching with no barriers, no sheaths. Him filling me, first with his dick and then his—.

Reid's eyes spark. "That turns you on, doesn't it?" He holds my hands tighter, then leans over to claim my lips in a scorching, quick kiss that sends my nerve endings blazing.

"I just want to be close to you."

"One day," he promises. "One day I'll enter you with nothing on. Just skin to skin. Just the two of us working against each other." His chest heaves in front of him. "Christ, Briar. How do you make me so hard every time? I didn't know you thought about things like that." He crushes his lips to mine, stealing my breath away. It's like we're at war now, him trying to massage every dirty thought I've ever had about him out, and me just trying to hold on, but not wanting him to win either.

He flips the lock on the door and leads me to the bed, pushing me forward until my hands are at the foot, spread out. His body hunkers around mine, hugging me from behind. But it's nothing as sweet as a hug. His one hand cups my breast through my shirt as his other runs down the crotch of my jeans. Before I know it, my knees are wobbly. He presses his hips into me, and I groan at the feel of how hard he is. He wasn't kidding with his statement earlier.

He works his hands around to my jeans, undoing the button and pulling them down until they fall around my ankles. His hands slip inside my panties without warning until he massages my clit. I arch back, and he pulls me against him. "Oh, God. This is going to be exactly like I imagined." He unclasps his jeans with one hand and pushes them down. I look between my legs to find his jeans and boxers off, his cock, now free, is resting against the thin barrier of my panties.

Reid kisses my shoulder, then moves his hand up my back, taking my shirt with it. I help him take it off. Once that's on the floor, he unclasps my bra, one-handed. I pull it free, dropping it on the bed ahead of us. His palm comes around to tease my nipples as his same hand still passes over my clit. "Reid," I breathe out. His unrelenting fingers working me up. "If you keep doing that, I'm going to come."

His body hugs me tighter, and he moves against me. He squeezes my nipple, pulling an excited cry from me, that I immediately try to stifle. "Don't hold back," he says. "Please."

His fingers continue to swirl against my clit until I can feel it coming. It's like he runs me right to the edge of a cliff and throws me over. My body clenches around nothing, but a silent cry falls from my lips as my fingernails dig into his comforter.

"That's my baby," he says, kissing my bare shoulder again. He hooks his fingers into my underwear and yanks down. His dick presses against me, and I move back, pressing into him, urging him to do whatever he has in mind.

I hear a condom wrapper rip open, and then his hands leave me while he puts it on.

When he comes back, he presses against my lower back. "Lean over more. Open your legs wider for me."

I do as he asks, and he caresses my ass, sliding his palm over it and squeezing.

"Push your ass into the air, Briar."

I do as he asks again. This time, I feel his cock sliding between my legs. I push my butt up higher until I feel him at my entrance. I start to tremble, my hands gripping his sheets between my fingers.

"Tell me if it hurts."

He pushes inside, and I cry out. *Hurt? Is he kidding?*

When he's fully seated, he groans, gripping my hip until it's almost painful. He doesn't move right away, like he's getting used to this new position, but eventually, his grip on me loosens and he starts pumping inside. It's a new sensation now that grabs ahold of my body. The noises Reid is making take the hotness of this to a whole other level. In no time at all, he's shaking. "Fuck me, Briar." He reaches around my hip to play with my clit, swirling his fingers over it with a frenzy. "I'm going to come," he says, his voice throaty and dark. I push back against him, relishing in the feeling of making Reid lose himself like this. "Shit, shit." His pressure on my clit intensifies. He's trying to make me come before he does, but he just can't contain himself. He bucks against me with a grunt, his fingers moving to my hips to hold me in place as he loses himself inside me.

"Oh God," I say as he barrels inside. His last few strokes drive me higher, but not enough to put me over the edge with him.

Reid groans, allowing himself a brief moment to enjoy his orgasm, but then he pulls out and pushes me forward, turning me until I'm on my back. He presses my knees to the bed and leans forward, stroking his tongue up my center. "You ready to come again, baby? You didn't think I was going to leave you hanging, did you?"

My fingers twist in his comforter while he flicks his tongue over my clit. I cry out, mesmerized by the way he's already fully tuned my body. I crave this. I crave him.

"Fuck that was amazing," he purrs.

His hand reaches up to tweak my nipples. My mouth opens in a silent scream.

"Tell me, Briar," Reid cajoles. "They can't hear you, I promise."

My breathing ratchets up. Short pants escape my mouth as he continues to tease my clit. "Reid, yes."

He moans his approval, sending vibrations through my sensitive core.

"Yes, please. Oh God."

The force of my orgasm pulls me off the bed. I sit up, staring down at his tongue stroking me as he pulls me closer to his mouth, forcing every last ounce of pleasure from me until I collapse back onto the bed.

He kisses up my stomach, chest, and eventually my neck before pulling me into his arms. Goosebumps crawl over my skin as I try to regain my composure. I turn to my side and nuzzle his chest, wishing for a moment that I didn't have to go home. That this could be our life. Except preferably without parental units downstairs either. For a moment, I wonder if this will be our future.

I turn onto my side and rest my head on his muscular bicep. "Reid?"

"Hmm?"

I phrase my next words carefully because the last thing I want is to make Reid feel like I'm clingy, but at the same time, I am being fucking clingy. "What's going to happen when we graduate?"

He turns toward me, then cusses under his breath, gets up to throw away the condom, and comes back. He pulls me close, his eyes glued to mine. "What do you mean?"

"Well, I know you want to go to Warner's."

"Yeah..."

I train my eyes on his chest. "I guess....well, I—."

He puts his finger under my chin and lifts my face to meet his. "You don't need to be uncomfortable around me. If this is about us going to school together. Yes, I fucking want you with me. Do I realize you have your own life to live?" His lips thin. "Yes, but fuck, Briar. This is real. All of it. Warner's is a good school. Hell, it's a great school. No, it's not ivy league, but you could do so well there." He runs his hands through my hair. "If all of that sounds anti-feminist, I'm sorry. I'm just speaking from the heart. I want to be with you. I want this, all day, every day."

A smile pulls at my lips. "It's on the downhill slide to anti-feminism, but I'll allow it because I want to be with you too."

He closes his eyes and sighs. Almost as if he's been worried about the same thing and not had the chance to bring it up with me yet.

I blink. "You were worried about it too?"

He half laughs. "I know how smart you are. I know you could go anywhere you want, so if you do decide to go to Warner's with me—if I get the scholarship and fucking Oscar doesn't take my spot—then I'll spend forever making it up to you."

I shake my head. "You don't have to make anything up to me. After Brady died, my priorities changed. Yes, I want to go to a good school and get a great job when we graduate, but you never know what's going to happen, right? As long as you're there, I'm there. That's what matters."

He nods his head knowingly. "Fate better not fuck with us because I'm all in."

The depth of his eyes, the earnestness in his voice, it makes my heart give a solid thump until his words are etched on my heart forever.

19

By the time Halloween rolls around, it feels like Reid might snap. I can tell by the set of his shoulders and the bags under his eyes that he never thought he'd be out of commission this long. If we even bring up football, his jaw starts ticking and his foot starts tapping. Reid and Lex barely even speak even though nothing has changed as far as how close they are physically to one another. The only thing that's happened since their fight is that Lex literally won't look at me anymore. He doesn't come around to make sure I'm okay. He doesn't ask me questions. He stares at his food during lunch, only speaking up when Cade says something.

I'll be fucking thrilled when the doctors okay Reid to start playing again. Not only will the hype around

Oscar die down, but Reid will get his spot back—and his confidence.

On Halloween, the guys have a game. Jules and I watch from the sidelines while Reid stands next to Coach, looking on stiffly as Oscar commands the field. He really is good. He's not better than Reid. He's not outplaying him, but it must feel that way to someone who can't even head out on the field and show everyone he can still do those things.

At the end of the second half, Reid storms to the locker room. Jules taps my leg, breathing out a breath that sounds like she's been keeping inside for a while. "He's a volcano waiting to erupt."

We both watch as Sasha throws herself into Oscar's arms, and they kiss like they have a semblance of privacy, which they don't. The team catcalls them, whistles and shouts galore as they follow far behind Reid to the locker rooms. Yes, even Sasha. She laces her arm through Oscar's and struts next to him like she belongs with the team. It must kill Reid to see her in there. To know what she did and not be able to say anything about it. To watch it all unfold when he can't do a damn thing.

"I've had about enough of this shit," I say, my fingers digging into my jeans. Not for the first time, I picture my fist connecting with her face, but other than some major satisfaction, what would that do? I need to think smarter. I definitely don't need to get kicked out of school for fighting. Not now when I have a goal to get into Warner's with Reid. He's even sweating the fact that they might want Oscar instead of him, but for me, I'll be pissed if missing school and running away and not caring about my grades stops me from going to college with Reid.

Eventually, Jules and I slowly make our way to Brady's little memorial. Last week, we planted some hearty mums in deep, fall colors. The more we wait, the more my stomach twists. The guys are usually out by now. I watch the door and see a few second and third-stringers creep out, heading for the parking lot. Tonight, there's a huge Halloween party being thrown at the same lake house Reid and Sasha broke up at.

Jules bumps my shoulder with her own. "Maybe you should go see what's going on..."

I meet her eyes and see the same concern etched there that's probably in mine. I know the guys can hold their own, but with Oscar and Sasha in there, I don't want things to boil over, not with the way Reid's been acting lately. "Yeah, I think you're right."

I start off down the paved walkway and end up on the other side of the locker room door. I've only come in here before with Reid ushering me in. Now, I'm by myself, so I pause, stare at it, and wonder what the hell I should do.

A metallic bang, like something hard hitting a locker, makes my decision for me. I pull on the door handle and step inside. Lex has Oscar pushed up against a row of lockers as the team watches. Sasha's at Oscar's side, tearing at Lex, her fingernails digging into his skin and leaving scratches. I stalk forward, catching Oscar's eyes first. His glint, like he knew something like this was going to happen. Like he was counting on it and wants to see how it all plays out, just like he told me before.

I yank on Sasha's arm, pulling her away from Lex. She stumbles back, falling into another player. "You bitch!" she calls out as soon as she sees it's me. Her lip curls as her gaze settles somewhere behind me.

"Lex, come on," I say, gently pulling on his arm across Oscar's throat. "He's not worth it."

It takes some more cajoling, but eventually, Cade steps in, and he and I move Lex away. Oscar stands up straight, running a hand down his bare chest. His hand finds his jeans, and he zips and buttons them. I look away, wondering what the hell sparked Lex to lose his shit in the middle of Oscar getting dressed. Honestly, it doesn't matter. The sight of those two makes every one of our hackles rise, so it's not surprising something ended up happening.

I turn, finding Reid sitting on a bench dressed in his track pants and school sweatshirt. Tension thickens the air, but at least the players who are still in the locker room go back to changing. I head toward him, his jaw hard. "Hey," I say, touching his arm. "You okay?"

He doesn't move. He doesn't even look up at me. He's so taut, he's close to snapping. The vibration of his anger scares me.

Cade comes over. "Just Sasha talking shit," he says, lowering his voice, so the only two people who can hear him are Reid and me. "Lex tried to shut her up, which got Oscar involved. Which prompted Oscar to say some shit about you. I think both these guys are ready to fucking lose it. Maybe we should just go to my house, see what my parents have in the liquor cabinet, and watch some horror movies."

I shrug. "Whatever everyone else wants." I honestly don't care about going to the party. My number one focus for the last couple of weeks has been Reid since it seems like he's slowly starting to lose it. I get it. To him, the life he always imagined is going up in flames around him.

"Hey, Baby, you hurt?" I hear a false sweet voice say behind us.

"Nothing you can't take care of."

I roll my eyes at the sound of Oscar's voice. We've come to a sort of truce in English in order to get our project done. We turn it in on Monday, so that's the end of that. Thankfully.

Her answering giggle is like nails on a chalkboard. "I'll do that thing you like." He growls playfully at her, and I make a sound of disgust, which only draws her attention. "What are you going to be for Halloween, Briar? A nun."

I shrug. "Not a bad idea."

Her gaze focuses behind me. I can see the switch to dark in her eyes, and I just know some seriously fucked up shit is about to come out of her mouth. "I bet Reid's getting a hand workout because of you. No wonder he can't play yet. You should try using the left, that way you don't work your hand out too much."

Oscar grabs his new Spring Hill hoodie out of his locker and pulls it on. When he turns his head, he glares at Sasha, but she doesn't notice. She's too busy trying to make it seem like Reid still should've chosen her. Yet, Oscar was right that one day in the library. Sasha will never get it.

Oscar glances at me, his expression unreadable,

then interlaces their fingers. "I think I have better things for your mouth to be doing, Sasha."

She sneers at us when we don't react. Oscar has to practically drag her out of the locker room. While he holds the door open for her, he looks over his shoulder at me, his lips turned down.

"Fuck that guy," Cade says as soon as he leaves. A few of the other players still in the locker room grunt in response. When I look around, I realize the place has almost emptied out. "He ain't shit."

"He's keeping up our winning season," Reid says, breaking his stoic trance to stand.

He seems taller than he usually is. Maybe it's the stiffness in his shoulders. I have to cock my head to look at him, hating that things aren't going the way they should be.

"And when you come back, *you'll* be keeping up our winning season," Cade shrugs. The faith he has in Reid makes a warm feeling spread through my limbs.

I wrap my arms around Reid, burying my head in his chest. Little by little, he softens, moving his arms around me. It's like he needs my presence to ground him, to show him that everything's not all bad because he still has me.

"So, my house?" Cade asks.

Reid shakes his head. "As much as I'd rather do

that, we can't. Well, I can't. I can't afford to. I need to be with the team. I can't let him take them away one-by-one so that it's awkward as shit when I come back. I have to show them I'm still their quarterback."

Cade looks away, moving discreetly out of the line of sight between Lex and Reid. Lex is sitting on the small bench in front of the row of lockers. I gasp when I see the small droplets of blood Sasha's fucking fingernail scratches gave him. I run to the bathroom, wet a paper towel, and come back out to wipe at his injuries. They're not serious, of course. Lex has seen a lot worse, but it looks like an annoying cat tried to get his attention for a few hours.

"I got it," he says, taking the wet paper towel from me.

"Which is why..." Reid says, his voice rising. "...when I go to handle my business, I don't need you stepping in for me."

Cade rubs the back of his neck, and I get the feeling that I definitely missed something.

Lex sighs. "I didn't know how it was going to go, and I didn't want your head to get hit, man."

"I don't fucking care about that."

"Oh, you don't fucking care about that?" Lex challenges. "I think that's all you fucking care about."

Cade steps between them. "Alright, alright. It was

a sucky night, okay? Can we just agree on that? Sasha's a bitch. Oscar's a dick. We don't need to let them interfere with what we've got going on."

"They're already interfering with what *I've* got going on," Reid says. "*Me.* He fucking took *my* spot. She fucking made sure it happened. Me. No one else. So, yes, I'll tell you what I want to happen because of it."

Cade's face changes. A shadow hovers over him, making it seem like he just stepped into a dark place. "You don't think that when she did that shit to you, she didn't also do that shit to us? Dude, we're a team. Always have been. Always will be. What happens to one of us happens to all of us."

Reid growls, the sound reverberating through the whole locker room. Turning, he slams his fist into the locker, making a dent. "It's not the fucking same."

Cade moves forward. He grabs Reid by the collar and pushes him against the locker he just made a dent in. "It is the fucking same. You're not going through it alone."

"Well, it fucking feels like it," Reid seethes. "I'm the one not playing on the field. I'm the one not helping the team. I'm the fucking one that might not get the scholarship. Oscar didn't come to take your fucking spots."

Cade shakes his head. "Get a fucking grip, Reid. And I mean that in the nicest of ways, but get a fucking handle on your shit. Stop ignoring Lex. Stop fighting with him. Stop this woe is me bullshit. I'm getting sick of it. None of us can say a goddamn thing anymore without wondering how you're going to react." He gives him another small shove into the locker and then backs away. "I'm going to my house. I don't feel like fucking partying tonight."

Cade grabs his jacket and slaps the locker room door, sending it crashing against the brick on the other side. I take my phone out and send Jules a text, asking her to make sure he's okay.

Lex stands when I put my phone away. His fist forms around the paper towel until water mixed with blood squeezes out and lands on the floor. "I need us to be okay, man. I don't want to tiptoe around you anymore." He gives me a quick glance. "I told you I'd back off, and I have. I don't know what more you want from me." When Reid doesn't answer him, he throws the towel away and leaves, leaving Reid and I alone.

Reid sinks to the floor, his hands coming up to run through his hair. I sit on the bench, facing him and the lockers, my legs straddling his knees. "You okay?" I ask.

"Depends," he says. "Are you going to yell at me too?"

I shake my head. "I wasn't planning on it."

His mouth quirks. "But you just might anyway?"

I shake my head. "No, Reid. I'm not going to yell at you. I don't think they were yelling at you either. I think they were just trying to tell you that they're there for you. In a way that you might finally hear it."

"That bad, huh?"

"I mean, you pissed Cade off. That's got to be saying something." I sigh when he doesn't laugh. "Come on. You know those three—two," I counter, quickly correcting myself. "You know those two would do anything for you."

Reid reaches up to put his hand in mine. "You can say three. I bet Brady's yelling at me right now, too."

I smirk. "He wasn't one to hold back, that's for sure."

After a moment, Reid says, "I just can't believe this is happening. Sometimes when I can't sleep, I stare at the ceiling and ask myself if this is fucking real life. I wonder if Sasha is actually one hundred percent certifiably crazy. Should she be in a legit fucking mental institution?"

"Yes, and yes."

Reid tugs on my hand, shaking his head at my answer. He keeps tugging until I land on top of him, his legs straightening out under the bench, so I can straddle him.

I hold his gaze. "The question is, what are we going to do about it?"

"What can we do? I just have to get better. That's what's going to stop all this."

"But won't she keep trying? Won't she not stop?"

"We can't control her crazy, Briar. We shouldn't even attempt to."

I blink at him, knowing he's making a hell of a lot of sense, but also thinking I don't quite agree with him. Someone has to teach her she doesn't fuck with us. There are consequences.

When Coach comes out of the back, he shoos us out of the room and instead of going to the party, we head to Reid's house to help his parents hand out candy.

20

On Monday, Oscar and I give our presentation on *The Great Gatsby*. Despite being unsure of our partnership in the beginning, we get an A, and that's literally all I wanted from him. When the bell rings, he reaches across the aisle and tugs on my shirt. I glance up at him, but instead of seeing someone who's about to say something cocky, I see a straight face. "I found him."

"Good for you," I say, having no idea what the hell he's talking about.

Oscar leans back in his chair, folding his arms over his chest. His foot comes to rest on the chair in front of him. "You're not interested in what I'm saying?"

"We really don't have a reason to talk anymore," I say, watching as the other students leave the room. "In case you weren't sure, that was us giving our presentation today. We got an A. Congratulations."

"You're cute when you're trying to be funny."

"Oh God, just stop talking."

"Gladly. What else can we be doing?"

I stand, pulling my bookbag on. "Bye, Oscar."

"Briar, wait," he says, scrambling up to meet me at the end of the aisle. "I found the dick that hurt Reid on purpose. I know where he hangs out. I know his number. It wasn't that hard to find, actually, so what I want to know is why you four haven't done the same thing?"

My mouth dries. I swallow, trying to keep what Reid said in my head. About us not having control of Sasha's crazy. But what if we can prove she paid this guy off to hurt Reid? Oscar was right about the pictures of me. No one cares. But this? They would both get into trouble. Lots of trouble.

"I can see the gleam in your eyes," he says, gloating. His usual dark eyes spark fire. It's unnerving how much this stuff excites him. "You want them to pay."

"Of course I do," I say through gritted teeth. "Who wouldn't?"

"I think you and I should pay him a visit."

"You and I?" I balk.

He gives me a look. "Call me crazy, but no one sees

you as a threat, Briar. That guy would walk all over you. But me? I'm from the Heights. That posh fucker will probably piss his pants. Remember how the guys from my neighborhood rolled up to Spring Hill? I'll do the same to him. I'll make him talk."

I chew on my lip. I don't know if I fancy myself a detective or what, but just the thought of getting this guy to admit what he did to Reid gives me goosebumps. Actually, I think it's the aftermath of what would come beyond the confession. Sasha would be in so much shit. *So* much shit. "Meet me after practice?"

A triumphant smile pulls Oscar's lips apart. "You got it. Lose the squares, and I'll take us there."

I roll my eyes internally. "What's Sasha going to think about this?"

"Fuck her," he says, his cheeks growing red even though he tries not to show it. "Maybe her spies will see us together, and she'll get raving jealous again. Jealous sex with her is fucking—"

I hold a hand up. "Right. Get it. Don't care."

"See you later, Page," he says as we go our separate ways when we walk out the door.

AFTER PRACTICE, I WAIT IN THE PARKING LOT

alone. It pays to have my mom trust Reid because my punishment has been all but lifted. All I have to do is text her back as soon as she texts me and keep her apprised of everything going on with Reid. It doesn't hurt that he comes over for dinner at least once a week. My parents like having him there. It's almost—*almost*—like having a Brady representative.

A whistle sounds at my back. I roll my eyes and turn, knowing I'll see Oscar there. I don't know how the hell he got away from Sasha for the evening, but I'm glad. He walks up to me, smirking.

"Tell me again why you're trying to help us."

His face falls. "Your boys helped me when I needed it. I'm just giving you a name, a location, and acting as the enforcer. You need to do all the talking."

"Actually," Cade says from behind him. "*We'll* be doing the talking."

Oscar turns, his shoulders sagging. He looks at me over his shoulder as Cade, Lex, and Reid approach. "Really?" The look on his face is actually hurt, like he wanted to spend some quality time alone with me roughing up some guy.

"We'll be doing the driving too," Lex says. He's still sweaty from practice, which makes him look a lot more intimidating than usual. "And the enforcing."

Reid flexes his fingers then tweaks them at Oscar in

a "give me" sign. "We'll be needing the info you have." When I approached them at lunch with the information Oscar found, he was the last one on board. Actually, I'm not sure it's the smartest thing for him to come either, but he has another doctor's appointment tomorrow, and I know he's trying to get his mind off that as much as possible. If this will help, I'm all for it. We don't need another replay of the guys fighting after they've all made up again.

Oscar shakes his head. "You guys aren't going to get shit from the guy."

Cade leans against Oscar's ride. It's a busted up piece of shit like the cars we saw the Rawley Heights guys show up in. I guess Sasha's help only goes so far since she's been driving to school in a BMW. "Tell me again why you're helping us."

"I told Briar already."

"I heard you," Cade says, "I just don't believe you."

"And I care about that why?"

"Sasha losing interest?" Lex asks.

"If you think I give a fuck about her, you're not paying attention. I'm sure Briar went running to you guys with the conversations we've had. I do things to help me out. You guys helped me out, I'm reciprocating. It's as easy as that."

"Does this mean next time your Heights buddies show up, we should let them beat your skull in?"

Oscar's eyes flash. There's a hint of fear there I haven't seen since his old teammates were lined up in front of the entrance to Spring Hill High. "I can hold my own with them."

"It looked like a mismatched fight to me," Cade says.

"That's the way we like it in the Heights." Oscar slides his gaze to me. He smiles like he can't believe this is happening, then scratches his jaw. "I suppose I can give you guys the information. I'll just text it to you, Briar."

Reid's nostrils flare. Oscar notices because, of course, that's the reaction he wanted out of him. He wants to make him jealous. Why? I don't understand. It's one of those things, I'm sure, where Oscar is looking out for himself and only himself. It's a shame. Maybe I've read him wrong, but Oscar just might not be that bad of a guy if he wasn't so interested in throwing elbows to the top.

Reid is right. We can't deal with other people's crazy. It's like that thing teachers say about keeping your eyes on your own paper. You can't control what other people do, but you can control what you do.

I give him my number and bring my phone out. "When you're ready," I say.

Oscar sighs, resigned. "All I know is his name and where the team hangs out after football practice. I suppose I could've found his address, but I didn't think I'd need it." He takes his phone out and texts me the information. I look down to make sure it's come in and then nod to the guys.

"Thanks," I tell him.

He glares at me and then at the rest of them. "You know, I wasn't there, but it seems weird how that fucker even got to Reid." His gaze drifts slowly to Lex. "Isn't that your job?"

"Fuck you," Lex says, his hands balling to fists. "Keep it up and next time I see a two hundred pounder swinging your way, I'll let them pass on by. Pretend I fucking slipped or something."

Oscar half smiles. "That's what I was looking for."

"Come on," Reid says. He's clearly done with this conversation. "Let's get a move on."

I forward Oscar's text to the rest of them, so we all have the information. Reid ushers us away from Oscar even though he thinks this is going to be a bust. He told us he thought it was a wild goose chase and that Oscar was just running his mouth. His gaze lingered on me too long to be a sweet gesture. Instead, it made my back bristle. When the bell rang to end lunch, he told me he thinks Oscar came up with this idea because he likes me.

I told him if that's what we needed to take Sasha down, I was okay with that. It can't hurt to have someone on the inside.

We all get into Reid's car, me in the front passenger seat and Lex and Cade in the back. "So, we're doing this?" Cade asks.

I turn around in my seat. "Yes, we're doing this," I say, shifting my gaze to Reid as he pulls out of his parking spot. "We need proof that Sasha did something fucked up. Getting her in trouble for spreading that picture of me wouldn't help because she hasn't denied she did it and has been showing others so they can pick on me."

"You mean Tiny Tits?" Cade helpfully says.

I slice a glare his way. "Yeah, that's it."

He holds his hands up. "I was just adding information to the conversation."

"But," I say, adding emphasis. "If we can get this guy to admit that Sasha literally paid him to take Reid out, someone would have to do something. It's like she put out a hit on him. Almost. Kind of."

Cade snickers.

Lex cracks his knuckles in his lap. "At the very

least, we could hold it over her head that we know what happened, so she doesn't do anything else to us. When Reid gets back on the team, she's definitely going to try something else."

I face forward in my seat again after locking eyes with Lex. I see the same worry I feel inside, swirling in the depths of his brown irises. We don't think Sasha is done with us. Not by a long shot. The only reason she hasn't done anything big yet is because things are going her way. Oscar's on the team, making Reid look like shit. She's shopped that picture around of me to anyone who will look. The comments I get in the hallway are proof enough of that.

But Lex's right. As soon as Reid takes back his spot, she's going to make another move.

21

The place Eli Richards hangs out after practice isn't too far from the school and the neighboring football field where Reid took his hit. My stomach clenches when we see it in the distance. I never want to go back to that day. I never want to have to worry about someone I love again.

Yes, that sounds naïve. I'm well aware. I can dream, though, can't I?

We walk inside, casually. At least, that's what I'm trying to do. My eyes dart around the players. Sure enough, Oscar was right about one thing. The guys inside this small cafe are all football players along with a few people dressed in business slacks like they're on their way home from work.

"Easy, Shortie," Cade says. He puts his hands on

my shoulders, and we head to a table in the corner. I hear words like yards, catch, and throw being tossed around, another reminder that we got the right place. "Be cool," he reminds me.

Lex and Cade go to sit on one side of the table, but I move in front of them. My eyes catch on someone who looks like it could be Eli to me, but his hair is a little different, so I want to watch him some more to be sure. When I saw him at the hotel room, he was more put together. Right now, this guy—if it is Eli Richards—is wearing a t-shirt with his team's mascot on it and a pair of sweatpants. When we saw him at the party, everything was so frenzied, but he looked like the guy from the hotel room right down to his designer jeans and nice shirt. I need to make sure we confront the right person because everything comes down to this.

"Okay..." Cade starts after I dart in front of him, his lips pulling apart like the next words out of his mouth are about to be something smartass.

"Leave her alone," Reid snaps.

We sit, and Cade leans forward. "What exactly is our plan? Are we just going to head over there and ask him if he ever took money to tackle someone before?"

He's got a point. For a hot second, I think we probably should've brought Oscar to help us figure this shit out. He knows how to be a sneaky bastard. This is his arena, not ours.

"I think that's him," I say, leaning back.

At the same time, Cade gets up. "I'll go get us some drinks. I'll take a look when I come back." He seems iffy about this whole thing. The only one completely on my side about all of this is Lex.

Lex sneaks a glance over his shoulder. "It's him." He turns sad eyes on me, and I remember he was there at the hotel room. He got just as good of a look as I did. "We can't discuss shit with him when he's got all his football buddies around him. There are only three of us."

"Four," I correct.

"Four," he says, giving me a small smile.

"Three," Reid says with finality, turning hard eyes to Lex.

I want to tell him if they're taking me out of commission, they may as well take him out of commission, too, but the last thing he needs is to be reminded that he has to take things easy.

A few minutes later, Cade comes back with four drinks. He drops them down in front of us like he's the waiter and slides into his seat. He shrugs. "Probably him."

"Well, I know it's him." I sneak my phone out,

zoom in, and snap a picture. Once I have it blown up on my screen, I turn it toward them. They all nod, and we bide our time as we wait for an opportunity to get Eli alone. A half hour passes, and nothing changes. They're all still sitting there until one guy gets up. Then, everyone in the room starts getting up. Before I can even move, Reid puts his hand on my leg. "Don't move. We'll walk out after them. Be cool."

My fingers tense on the table. I swear if one of them tells me to be cool again... Were they cool when they went all caveman on me in the beginning of the year?

I take a deep breath, holding it inside until every last guy from the cafe has left. Gripping the seat beneath me, I wait until the others start moving. First, Cade casually gets up. Reid follows, so I stand, too, slipping my hand through his. He takes mine gently, like it's any other day.

Lex pushes the door open, and we all follow him outside onto the cracked sidewalk littered with changing leaves. I follow Cade and Lex blindly. I'm too short to see over them, and they're too wide for me to see between them. Up ahead, I hear voices, and suddenly, Lex and Cade move to the side. They lean casually against the building, and Reid pulls back on my hand, so we both come to a stop in front of them.

"What the fuck is *he* doing here?" Lex asks, sliding a stormy glance in the direction we were headed.

"Fuck," Reid spits. "Oscar?"

I don't dare look over because I don't want to be conspicuous and because I'm supposed to "be cool."

Cade nods slightly. "He's talking to our boy."

"I swear to God I'm going to fuck him up," Reid says. I can hear the growly nature in his voice and the tense lines of his hand that's still in mine.

Lex shifts so he can get a full-on look at what's happening. His lips move into a thin line as he watches beyond us with a level of concentration I recognize from the football field. I guess that's kind of what we're doing here. We're running a play. Trying to score some points by sneaking past others... Or maybe I really do need to calm the fuck down. "Jesus," Lex sighs. The lines at the corners of his eyes tighten. "They're leaving. The team," he says quickly. "Not Oscar and Eli."

I hear a few cars start up and see some drive down the street past us shortly afterward.

"They just disappeared around the corner of the building."

This spurs everyone to move. Lex first, then Cade. Reid pulls me behind him while still keeping his hand latched securely in mine. When we come around the side of the building, I see Oscar and Eli talking like it could be any conversation, but when Eli turns to see us, he goes from curious gaze to wide eyes in a nanosecond. "Fuck."

He tries to make a run for it, but we—the five of us, Oscar included—close ranks around him until Eli's back is pressed against the side of the brick building and we've formed a semi-circle around him. "Not getting away this time," Lex says.

Eli turns to Oscar. "You fucker."

Oscar just shrugs and puts on one of his devilish grins. "Well, I really did need to talk to you, and technically, it kind of is about Sasha. I didn't lie about everything."

"I don't know what you're talking about," Eli says. He turns to Reid. "I haven't looked at your girl. Not once. I haven't touched her, looked at her, thought about her..."

Reid's green eyes flare. "We're not here about that. What I want is proof you and Sasha scheming tried to take me out. You got text messages implicating Sasha's dirty ass in this shit, or are we just going to kick your ass? It's long fucking overdue." He lets go of my hand and crosses his arms over his chest. His intimidation factor just went up a hundred degrees. Oddly, so did his sexiness factor.

"I told you I was done with this shit," Eli tries

again. He has a long, thin nose and super gelled dark hair. "I told you her parents were going to throw me in jail. Besides, a tackle's a tackle. You don't need to be a bitch about it."

Reid, Lex, and Cade step in closer, so I follow suit. "A fair hit's a fair hit," Lex says. "What you did was fucked up. I know it wasn't just you on my QB, and I also know it wasn't your idea. But don't stand there and tell me you're just a victim in all this."

"I'm not looking to get you in trouble," Reid says, the shadows on his face darkening. "You're right. It was out on the field. A hit's a hit. You sacked me fair and square. I want to know Sasha's involvement. I don't give a shit about you unless it's to beat your ass like I should have that night at the party for fucking with my girl."

I feel Oscar's eyes settle on me. It makes a tickle of unease settle in the back of my neck. He didn't know about the hotel room and what Richards and Sasha tried to do.

Reid continues. "And don't think that by not talking you're sparing Sasha either. She gives as many fucks about you as I do."

Eli runs his hands through his hair. His gaze darts behind us like he wishes his football buddies would come back. I hope they don't.

"I was hoping I wouldn't have to do this..." Oscar stalks away from the group. I watch him as he moves to his car, which I now notice is parked on the street a few down. He opens up the back door and brings out a baseball bat.

"Aw, fuck," Eli says, teeth clenched.

Cade lifts his eyebrows, but turns his attention back to Eli. "You know he's from Heights, right? I don't think he's playing. He doesn't give a fuck about playing fair."

"If I get shit..." Eli starts.

Oscar's voice carries over to us on his way back to the group. "We both know Sasha hasn't contacted you since she got me."

"The team's everything to me, man," Eli says, eyeing Oscar the entire time as he moves back into the group, the bat lying on his shoulder all casual-like.

"I said I wasn't interested in getting you," Reid says. "If you ask me, Sasha needs to get taken down. She thinks she can get whatever she wants whenever she wants. She played you. She played me. She's playing Oscar."

I sneak a peek at Oscar, but his face is made of stone. His fingers are white-knuckling the grip on the bat like he could take a swing at any moment.

I never thought about how convenient a bat might

be in a fight. And here all I have is pepper spray to warn off an attacker.

Oscar sighs. "Did I mention my patience sucks?" He turns toward the rest of us. "Fuck this. He's not talking." He raises the bat and takes a step forward, bringing it back like he's about to swing for the fences.

"Fuck, fuck. Okay!" Eli's nostrils flare, his hands outstretched. "She asked me to hit you hard. She wanted you to get injured. I wore a weighted vest, even had weighted metal wrapped around my forearms and went right for your helmet with it. Okay? Fuck!"

"That was the fucking noise I heard," Lex growls. "You piece of shit." Lex steps toward him, his fist moving back.

Eli brings his hands up in front of his face when Oscar also takes a menacing step forward again. "Where I come from, we get retribution for that fucked up pussy shit."

Cade holds his hand out to stop Oscar and Lex. My stomach clenches as I study Oscar's profile. It looks like he's out for his own blood, like he has a personal stake in the matter and not like he's doing this for someone he came to Spring Hill to ruin, anyway. But like he's said before, he's a man of opportunity. Maybe he's more like a man who just likes bloodshed and fear.

Reid steps closer. "Listen to me, you fucking

asshole. I haven't been able to play since you gave me that hit. I've got some fucking clown in my spot, and I'm not leaving here until you make it right one way or another. Either we kick your fucking ass. Or you give me something to use on Sasha. Since I'm guessing you like to play as much as I do, I'll give you the courtesy you didn't give me. Look through your fucking cell. Find me something."

My mouth dries. I watch the thinly veiled anger seethe through Reid, settling in the tight lines of his back. In front of him, Eli pulls out his phone and starts pressing the screen frantically. Finally, he says, "Here. Here's something."

We press in tighter as Reid turns to read what it says. He takes his phone out and takes a picture of Eli's screen. "More."

Eli bites his lips, scrolling furiously through what must be hundreds of texts from Sasha. It's probably full of fake drivel, but if they were stupid enough to talk about it, all the better. "Here," Eli says again, showing him something else.

Reid takes another picture with his phone, then instructs Eli to hold it next to his face, so he can take a picture of Eli and the screen at the same time. The dude's positively white and shaking. He should be.

"Perfect," Cade says, smiling. "That and the audio I took of all this should be enough."

Eli sighs, but I glance over at Cade appreciatively. These guys are way better at this than me. He probably recorded the whole damn conversation.

We start to move away, but Reid stays. "A word of advice? Doing things like that for someone like her just makes you her bitch, not her hero." He gives him one good shove against the brick building, and we all move away.

The four of us turn toward Reid's vehicle. I don't even think twice about Oscar until I hear him say, "Uh, you're welcome!"

Reid and Cade both lift their middle fingers without glancing back. I turn my head quickly to find Oscar staring me down. I don't give him anything though. I just turn right back and hop in Reid's car, grateful I've got friends like these.

I hold my hand out, demanding Reid's phone from him. After he presses it into my palm, I lean between the seats and Cade and Lex lean forward to get a view. There it is. Somewhat what we wanted. In one message, it's Sasha asking Eli if he can do her a favor involving "that egotistical dick who went slumming". I shake that off. It's the next one that matters most, anyway. Sasha asks Eli if he's ready for tonight. The date clearly reads the day Reid got hit. Eli replies, GOT MY VEST AND WEIGHT PLATES TO GO UNDER MY ARM GUARDS. BOUT TO PUT THE HURT ON.

Yeah, he's not very smart. In a way, I feel bad for him. He's just dumb and easily manipulated. But then I remember he gave the guy I love a fucking concussion and was down to take dirty pictures of me, so that's about as far as that goes.

In the last text box on the phone is Sasha's response: YOUR REWARD along with a tongue emoji and a plethora of eggplant emojis.

And so, now we know Eli did all this for some head.

22

The next day at school, Oscar avoids me. Not that I was looking for deep, meaningful conversation with him, but he went out of his way to not even look at me. A sense of relief filters through my whole body with a strange hint of fear. I didn't want to be on Oscar's radar, but at the same time, I don't want to be his enemy either. I saw the look in his eyes when he had the baseball bat in his hands and stalked toward Eli. I don't ever want to be on the receiving end of that.

Reid isn't at school all morning. The texts I send him go unanswered until he waltzes into the cafeteria during lunch only five minutes after the bell has rung. I can't tell from his face if he got good news or bad news. He has that passive indifferent look. The one that makes him look aloof to all his surroundings. It helps him out on the field, but personally, I prefer the way he smiles at me.

"So?" Cade asks when Reid sits next to me.

Reid bumps my shoulder. My heart's in my throat. There's this weird pent up vibration coming off him that I can't quite place. He slowly turns toward me. I swear it takes several long seconds, his green eyes swirling, but eventually, the corners of his mouth lifts. "He signed off."

I gasp. "Seriously?"

I hear Cade and Lex congratulate him in the background, but Reid's only looking at me, and I'm only looking at him. I lean forward, pressing my lips to his. He takes the kiss deeper, and it might just all be in my imagination, but this kiss, it's more confident. It's not as needy or as wild as it has been. It's skilled and articulate until I have to pull away because it's just way too much for the lunch room.

Cade nods knowingly when my gaze drifts to him, and I feel my face heat like a furnace.

Lex turns back toward us, his shoulders stiff. He relaxes some when he realizes we're not kissing anymore. "Well?"

"Just got back from seeing Coach," Reid says. "I'm starting next game."

Lex and Cade move in. All the other players sitting at the opposite end of the table from us aren't paying attention. "Fuck yes," Cade whispers. "I knew he'd put you back in."

Reid shifts. I can tell he was unsure what Coach would do. Oscar has been doing a really good job. "He told me I've been his QB since I was a sophomore, and he's not going to turn his back on me now."

"Coach must've been happy," Lex says.

Reid leans back and puts his arm around my shoulders. "Not as happy as me."

It feels good to have Reid be this positive again. I left him at his worst. When I came back, he was a little better, but not the Reid I grew up with. Not the one I was with when we first got together. Football was missing for him, and if I didn't already know what a big piece of his life football was, I'd know it now. Tension starts to ease in my stomach, but it doesn't last.

Lex leans forward even further, signaling the rest of us to get in close, too. "This means Sasha's going to be out for you again, man," Lex tells Reid, holding his gaze. "She's not going to let it drop. Her guy won't be quarterback anymore, which is going to piss her off. We need to figure out what the fuck we're going to do with the information we got yesterday. Fast."

"Is Coach announcing it during tonight's practice?" Cade asks.

Reid nods. "He's going to pull Oscar aside first, then he's telling the whole team."

"Which means Sasha will know right after practice," Lex says. His gaze switches from me to Reid. "Shit's going to get worse. She's already shown she's capable of some fucked up shit."

Reid shakes off the intensity of our gazes. "I'll just tell her I have shit on her and to back the fuck off. The minute she comes after either one of us, I'll tell everyone what I know."

"We could just tell everyone now," I say. "Why wait? If we tell everyone now, she'll get in trouble."

"But she could still retaliate," Lex says. His gaze softens when it meets mine. It's as if he feels sorry for going against my idea.

"I agree," Reid says. "As long as we have something over her, it might keep her in line. Let's just see how the talk I have with her goes. We'll know more what to do after that. Whether we scare her enough to keep her in line, or if she's just that stupid and crazy to try something."

Every time Reid talks about Sasha I see a hint of something in his eyes. It's not regret of not having her anymore. I know Reid loves me. He doesn't miss her.

He hates her. But I don't understand what the vibe I get off him is. Reid did like her once upon a time. If I put myself in his shoes, I'd be wondering how someone I trusted could've turned on me like this. To go out of their way to hurt me. Maybe that's what it is. A disbelief in how crazy this chick actually is.

Jules sits down a moment later, and we bring her up to speed. The guys talk to her as if she's one of them—one of us. I hope that's the case. Brady was her world. If she didn't have us, she wouldn't have anyone right now. She looks at Reid. "I'm so glad you're starting again." A small smile filters over her face, and then she goes quiet for the rest of the period, lost in her own thoughts.

When I see her a couple of periods later, we decide to watch practice tonight. We don't want to miss the show if there's going to be one. How Sasha's going to react. Hell, how Oscar's going to react to hearing the news. In my head, I still see the angry guy. The one who puffed up in front of his Heights buddies on campus and the one who strode toward Eli with the evil glint in his eye, but I've seen other parts of him too. I'm not saying he's a good guy. Not at all. But I'm saying I think he's doing what he thinks he needs to do to survive. The fact that he came to Spring Hill to start for the team—a position he thought was secure—is now going to be over... It's going to crush him. He wants the All-State Scholarship as much as Reid, and he thought Spring Hill was his ticket.

All the way until practice starts, I'm plagued with worry over how Oscar's going to deal with the news. Not all because I feel sorry for him, but because if he loses his shit and hurts Reid, I don't know what the heck we'll do. Why do bodies have to be so brittle? One wrong move and Reid could get hurt again. One tackle and Brady loses his life. Like, Christ, maybe we should all be running around in plastic bubbles.

I see Reid right before practice and give him a big hug before walking out to the stands with Jules. The cheerleaders are already there, practicing a pyramid. Sasha's high-pitched screech rings around the field as she scolds two of the base girls. I swear she's a tyrant. How anyone can stand her is beyond me.

"What do you think she's going to do?" Jules asks.

"I don't know, but it won't be good," I say, echoing the thoughts I've been thinking all afternoon. "She thinks she runs the school. Everything she does hasn't told her any differently. She totally played Reid by bringing Oscar in and dating him, like he was some sort of Reid substitute."

"That guy gives me the creeps," Jules says, a shiver running through her.

I don't say anything. Not that I don't agree with her. I do. He's a dick, and he's admitted to me multiple times that he's just in it for himself. But, I can't help but think that if Oscar grew up in Spring Hill, he might've been welcomed into Cade, Lex, Reid, and Brady's pack. Like they could've been five best friends instead of four. It's clear he takes football as seriously as the guys do. He has to if he can even step in to Reid's shoes and fill them.

As if on cue, the door to the locker room opens, and the team starts running out. Reid leads the way. He's got his game face on, but I can tell he's pleased. Sasha watches with a scowl during a break in cheerleading practice. And Oscar, well, he's jogging behind the rest of the team. His face is impassive, but tight. The corners of his eyes are stretched a little too tight to be anything but worry or anxiety. He didn't take the news well, but he hasn't done anything about it either. I don't know what I expected. A trip to his car, so he can get his baseball out and beat Reid with it? That wouldn't be subtle at all, but it would put him back in the starting position.

Then again, he wouldn't have had the chance to do it right before practice. That's something that's done in a dark alley, not surrounded by others. Especially coaches and teammates who can identify you. No,

Oscar's smarter than that. He wouldn't let his rage get the better of him.

Jules bumps her shoulder into mine. "You okay?"

I let out a breath I hadn't realized I'd been holding. "Just worrying about everything, I guess." I run a hand down my face. "Oscar and Sasha. That's a terrible twosome if I've ever seen one. I think they're both willing to go to whatever lengths necessary to get what they want. Even Oscar himself told me to think bigger when I wanted to get dirt on Sasha—a girl he's supposedly seeing."

"I don't think seeing is the right word for it," Jules says, eyeing everyone move onto the field. "Partners in crime, maybe. Or just fuck buddies."

She's not wrong about that. Oscar doesn't really care about her. He's said so himself. The only nice thing he's ever said about her is that she's good in bed. Not sure that's the best quality in a person, but to each their own. He's not here for Sasha at all. He's here for himself.

The whole practice, Reid doesn't look rusty at all. His game is on point, and he knows it. He's on top of the world. The only bad thing about him practicing in the quarterback position is that Sasha knows something's up. She doesn't even have to hear it from Oscar first. She's glaring at the field for the rest of practice and even dismisses squad practice early. She sits on the bottom bleacher, waiting for practice to end.

When it does, I lose her and Oscar for a bit because Reid's beckoning me to come see him. I look for Sasha again, but don't see her, so I make my way down the bleachers and meet Reid at the gate in the fence. "That felt fucking amazing," he says. His green eyes glitter with exhaustion and excitement.

"You don't feel out of sorts or anything?" As I ask that, I realize he wouldn't. He doesn't get tackled on the field during practice. They don't take the risk of him getting injured. The real test will be the game. I just have to pray he doesn't get hit. My eyes immediately move to Lex. He's sucking down water out of a green bottle. When he polishes it off, he throws it to the side. I don't even need to tell him to watch Reid like a hawk. He'll do it, anyway. Reid kisses the side of my forehead. "I'm going to shower and dress, let's go out with the guys tonight. Pizza or something. Text your mom you'll be with me." He turns to Jules. "You, too."

With that, he jogs off. Jules laughs at me while I stare after him. I can't help it. He always looks hot right after practice. "I'll have to pass on pizza tonight. I already promised Mom I'd go shopping with her."

I turn toward her and smile. "Tell your mom I said

hi. Maybe when the football season is over, I can make it out to your house."

"She'd love that."

I give Jules a quick hug, holding her tight for a brief second before letting go.

I make my way to the side locker room entrance while sending my mom a text that I'm going to get pizza with Reid and the team. My phone buzzes back with a response when I get to the door, but a growl grabs my attention. It isn't an animal, but a male human. I move to the edge of the school and peek around the corner of the building. I move back as soon as I see Oscar and Sasha there. Whatever caught my attention before, I can't hear anything now. It's obvious Oscar is furious. I peek back around. He's in Sasha's face. I can tell she's trying to stand tall, but she seems to shrink in his presence.

Sasha says something back, and Oscar lunges for her. I gasp, pulling back around the side of the building, my heart in my throat. I stay there with my eyes closed for a few seconds and then sneak a peek back around the brick. Oscar has his forearm wedged under her chin, pushing into her throat. She's pushed against the side of the building, and he's in her face again, their noses practically touching. He says one last thing to her and then pushes off. He looks up, his gaze wild, fury filtering through his features like an angry landscape. I move back, but not before he looks right at me.

I close my eyes for a brief second and blow a breath out. When I open my eyes again, he's standing in front of me, his shoulders heaving with big, angry breaths. "I guess you must be pretty happy today."

I nod once. I don't know how much to give away. He's not looking at me like he was looking at Sasha. He seems kind of resigned, with a flicker of anger here and there. When I don't say anything, Oscar goes to walk into the locker room, but I reach out for him, grabbing the sleeve of his shirt. "Wait," I say. He turns toward me. His gaze starting on where my fingers still hold on to his shirt and follow my arm all the way up to my shoulders and then finally my face. I swallow. "Don't hurt him, Oscar." My throat feels like it's about to close in on me, but I let go of him and push my chin slightly into the air. "Don't hurt Reid."

Amusement passes over his face, but he looks more annoyed than anything. "You're scared of me, aren't you, Page?"

I shake my head no. And in that moment, I'm not lying. Oscar is someone who's had to do the things he's done because of where he grew up. Life was hard, so he was harder. His friends were tough, so he was tougher. His enemies were evil, so he plays by the devil's rules. "I'm not scared of you, Oscar. I'm scared of what that voice inside your head is telling you to do."

He steps forward, and I take a step back. He does it again with the same reaction. And then again, but this time, I'm up against the building with nowhere else to move, so he's in front of me, the tips of our shoes almost touching. I can feel his breath on my face. "You see so much," he says. He runs his hands through his hair, making it spike up. "You're ten times the woman Sasha will ever be. If only you weren't afraid of me, Briar."

"I'm not afraid," I say again.

The corner of his mouth quirks up, and he steps back. "I can't promise you I won't hurt him. I can promise I won't ever hurt you though. You're the only thing in Spring Hill I like besides football." With that, he turns and pulls open the locker room door, disappearing inside.

23

The rest of the week goes by quickly. Reid's determined to have a huge comeback out on the field, so he's been preoccupied since making it back as the starter on the team. Oscar and Sasha have both been lying low, though we all notice how Sasha stares our way during lunch. Oscar and Sasha are never around each other anymore though. They don't parade in front of the school anymore like they're the "it" couple. In fact, none of us have seen them in the same room with the other since I saw them arguing outside the school after practice.

The morning of the game, Reid sends me a text. **The moment you came back to me, I thought anything was possible. Thank you for giving that to me.**

My heart practically melts on the floor. No one would know that Reid has a sweet side. He's a big, burly football player that likes winning and has a tendency to think he's better than most people. I happen to think he is better than most people, so I'm not going to argue with him there, but all the heartfelt words and caring gestures, they're only for me.

My nerves are shot by the time I get to the game. Both Jules and I stop by Brady's memorial before the game starts. We're silent as we stand outside it. I don't know what Jules talks to Brady about when we come here, but I usually tell him about everything that's been going on. Today, though, I'm asking him to take care of Reid. I want him to look out for him, to make sure if he gets tackled that he gets right back up.

On our way to the stands, Jules loops her arm in mine. "He's going to be fine."

"He better be."

"If he isn't, you're not leaving again," she says. I lift my head to look at her. "I mean it, Briar. I will pin your ass down."

She's serious as hell, but I laugh anyway. "I'm not leaving again. I promised already."

There's a buzz in the stands. It's almost palpable. Reid's comeback was on the front page of our small town's paper, and the stands seem even fuller than they were when Reid was playing before.

Everyone likes a comeback story.

When the team runs out onto the field, they get a standing ovation. The applause seems louder, the excitement builds higher. I can't help but think that there's a little extra in there for Reid Parker. I'm sure he's loving the shit out of this.

He looks into the stands and finds me here. We keep one another's gaze, not moving, definitely not talking, but we seem to know what the other is thinking and feeling, anyway. Right before he looks away, I smile and so does he.

I track Oscar down next. He's standing next to a player on the team who hardly ever plays. They both have their uniforms on, but it strikes me that I want Oscar's looking just as pristine as it does right now by the end of this game. I couldn't get him to promise not to hurt Reid, but he did promise not to hurt me. He has to know that hurting Reid would hurt me. And whatever kind of person he is, I don't see him doing that.

My gaze moves away from him and focuses on Sasha. She's busy cheering with her squad, but everything with her is a facade. She was doing the same thing the day she paid Eli to hurt Reid. She could have the same thing in store for him today while she simultaneously roots for the team through cheers and pompoms. She's like a gift that holds a severed heart. It looks good on the outside, but inside, you know exactly what the meaning is.

When I look away from her, I catch Lex. He's standing next to the bench, re-tying his cleats. He does that before every game. It's an OCD thing for him. He ties them once in the locker room and then once more while they're out on the sidelines waiting for the game to start. He meets my stare and nods.

That's all I needed. He's got this under control. No one's getting a hit on Reid tonight. No way.

As if following my train of thought, Jules says, "Lex looks like he's all business today. I don't think he'll be letting anyone by him. He might snap if the ref even gets too close."

I laugh at that. They've always protected each other that way their whole lives. Just because someone got by Lex once, doesn't mean a thing. Oscar implied Lex did it on purpose. That's only because that's what he's used to in his world. These boys, they would never do that to each other.

As the minutes tick by on the game clock, it's obvious the game is going to be a complete blowout.

Spring Hill's offense is on point with Reid taking the reins. Every time they get the ball back, they march down the field like there isn't even a defense in between them and their touchdown. Reid is charged up throughout. He chest bumps his O-line, he slaps their hands, and when the offense runs off the field to make way for the punting team, Coach is in Reid's face and smacking him on the side of the head in congratulations. I wish Warner's had sent scouts tonight. He's playing amazingly. Like he owns this turf and this team.

I can't help but to find Oscar on the sidelines. The more points we score, the tenser he gets. He claps along with the rest of the team, but he never goes over to Reid to pump him up or tell him how good he's playing. Oscar just looks like a casual observer. Hell, he could be watching from right next to me in the stands and no one would know the difference. It's like he's yesterday's news.

Right before the last play of the game, I make my way down to the chain-link fence that separates the team from the crowd. The opposing team had one last chance to score, but we stopped them. I'm just starting to smile and clap, relief sweeping through me that Reid made it out just fine, when a body moves into view. I look up to find Oscar moving toward me. I still and watch him warily as he tracks right up to me. Just like I'd wanted, his uniform hasn't even been scuffed up. Hell, he's not even sweating. He's still holding his helmet in his hands. "What are you going to do with the information you found out?" He drifts his eyes toward where the cheerleading squad is completing their last cheer, making it clear he knows who I'm talking about.

I shrug. "Why do you care?"

He leans forward, his face tense. "You forget I'm the reason you found out that information, and right now, I want to take that bitch out so bad I can't fucking stand it. So, tell me your little bitch ass friends are going to serve her what's coming to her, or I'm going to have to dish out her punishment."

His words make a tingle of apprehension slither its way up my spine. "Is that supposed to scare me?" I ask. "You know she hurt the guy I love. Why the hell would you think I care what happens to her?"

Oscar scowls. "Because my punishment will be much more physical. I won't just be taking her down, I'll be taking her out. You understand me, Page?"

Despite myself, I feel the tiniest bit of concern for the girl. I saw how Oscar acted outside the locker room.

Imagine him trying to hurt her? "I understand you," I tell him, keeping my voice even.

Shadows pass over Oscar's face. "She fucked me over."

"She fucks a lot of people over." I look around him to see Reid still celebrating with his team. "You should think about not fucking yourself over in the process of getting back at her."

He tilts his head, his dark gaze swimming with emotion. He opens his mouth to say something, but Reid's voice calls out from behind, "Excuse me, Drego." He moves in beside him, lowering his hands over to my side of the fence. I think he just wants to hug me, but instead, he steps up into the fence, sliding his hands under my armpits, and lifts. Before I know it, I'm being pulled to the other side. I lift my feet and tuck them around Reid's waist. His shoulder pads are big and uncomfortable, but I throw my arms around him, anyway. "Hey, Baby," he whispers into my neck.

A flush of heat swamps me. "You did it."

He laughs, the sound ringing around us. "Was there ever any doubt?"

His green eyes spark, lifting hesitation off me. Hesitation about him playing again. Fear of Sasha and Oscar going after him. I know he can handle himself, so for the time being, I let those worries slip away and just be the quarterback's girlfriend after he's had—arguably—the best game of his career. "No," I tell him simply. "Never."

When Reid finally sets me on my feet, Oscar is gone. Reid's parents call us over to the gate in the fence, and when he walks out, his mother wraps him in a fierce hug. One I have to even let go of his hand for, so he can return it.

"Great job, Son," Mr. Parker says. "Solid playing."

"I'm just glad you're okay," Mrs. Parker says. Her eyes are glistening like she's close to tears or has already been crying intermittently through the entire game.

He gives her shoulder a squeeze. "I'm fine, Mom."

She gives him one more hug and then they tell him they'll see him at home. We wave bye, and Reid takes my hand again right before Jules strolls up. She tells Reid how great he played and then tells us she plans on going to the party tonight, but needs to go home first.

"Jeez, I forgot about the party," I say, annoyance settling in. I want Reid to myself right now.

Reid squeezes me.

"Since your man is back to number one at Spring Hill, I'm sure you'll be going," Jules teases before she waves and heads back down the path to the parking lot.

The football field and surrounding areas are almost vacant now. The last stragglers of the team, including

Cade and Lex, are just now getting to the locker room door. I expect Reid to head that way, but instead, he takes me around the front of the building.

"What are you doing?"

"Shh," he says, a huge smile taking over his face.

When we step inside the school, he pulls me immediately to the boys' locker room. All the guys are in the front, talking about the game, so they don't hear us come in. He pulls on my hand and walks toward the supply closet. "Reid," I say in disbelief. I'm not going to say I'm not tempted, but the last time we did this, we were all alone. The whole freaking team is in the locker room right now.

"Come on," he says. The door opens easily in his hand, swinging outward without a sound. Before I know it, I'm being ushered inside. It's even darker in here than I remember it being, but that's the last rational thought I have until Reid's hand grips me. "I can't wait," he says. He presses me against the back of the door, his hot breath on my face. "We're going to be at the party soon, and I'm going to have to stick around when all I really want to do is drag you up to an upstairs bedroom."

He kisses a trail down my neck. His pads are bulky, but on the other hand, I've always thought he looks sexier than hell in them. It doesn't take me long to be totally on board with this idea.

Reid's hand sneaks under my shirt. His touch sprouts goosebumps until his thumb traces over my bra, my nipple pebbling underneath it. I moan low in my throat, but Reid stills. His head picks up. His reaction makes me alert, and I strain to hear what's stopped him. It doesn't take long to figure out what's got Reid intrigued.

"Coach—" It's Oscar talking. Reid moves away from me after pulling my shirt back down.

"I'm sorry, Drego. There's nothing I can do for you. I can't play you when my number one QB for two years is ready and able. Not only that, he's killing it out there. You've got to see that."

Silence from Oscar.

"Listen, the team and I were so glad you showed up when you did. I don't know how you came here with such perfect timing, but you helped Spring Hill out when we needed it." There's a few seconds gap before Coach says, "What if I put you in as a wide receiver? How are your hands?"

"The All-State, Coach," Oscar tries to argue.

"The All-State looks at all players, not just QB's. Playing in any position still makes you eligible. What doesn't make you eligible is sitting on the damn sidelines. Now, come on. I know you have a warrior spirit. You're not meant to ride the bench, Drego. I understand it's not the position you want, but it's yours if you want it."

I clench up. I know exactly whose position Coach is trying to give him. Not that I blame Coach. He needs a player, and Oscar's good.

"I'm a quarterback," Oscar says through clenched teeth.

"Not for Spring Hill, you aren't. Not while Reid Parker can play." Coach sighs after a moment. I freeze at how close they must be. They're literally on the other side of the door. If I hit one thing, our cover is blown, and they're both going to know what we're doing in this room. I don't even know if there's anything around me that I could accidentally bump into, but I'm not taking the risk. I'm staying right where I am. "Come on, Drego. I'm giving you an opportunity here. Even not at quarterback, you know they'll watch you more if you're here and not back at Rawley Heights."

"I can't go back to Rawley Heights," Oscar says, voice dropping.

He's not kidding. He'll definitely get his ass kicked there. The guys that showed up at Spring Hill were serious.

"Then it's settled," Coach says. "Come Monday, I want you practicing with the wide receivers. Okay?"

A knot forms in my stomach. *Oscar playing in my brother's spot now? What next?*

Footsteps sound beyond the door like one of them has started to walk away. Oscar says, "Sure thing, Coach. But your Golden Boy? You might want to check out his story."

Then, the footsteps start up again and disappear. I look at Reid, who's staring at the door with thin lips.

Check on Reid's story? What the hell does he mean by that?

THE PARTY ISN'T REALLY MUCH OF A PARTY. Not for me, anyway. Ever since Reid and I overheard Oscar and Coach Jackson talking, Reid's been in a mood. We didn't finish what we started when Coach left the back area of the locker room. Not even close. Instead, Reid opened the door, sat me on the bench and went into the main area of the locker room to shower and change without another word.

While he's in there, I keep wondering what the hell Oscar was talking about. What *story* is he referring to?

Whatever it is, it's probably all bullshit. Oscar's

pissed. And I can see why. Yes, he was the fucker who Sasha brought in to take Reid's spot, but from his point of view, everything just got pulled out from underneath him. I think back to the conversation we had over the fence and wonder if he really will try to get Sasha. I imagine he will, but there's one thing I can't see him doing, and that's hitting her with that bat. I don't know why. I know he's not a good guy. I know he's done questionable things, but I don't see him doing *that*.

Maybe it's me seeing him in my brother and Reid, and in Lex and Cade, too.

Cade's the one who comes back to get me. "Come on, Shortie. We're about to go celebrate." He's got sunglasses on and a white button-up shirt with the top buttons open. He only has one side of his shirt tucked into his jeans. The other is fashionably out, making him look like he didn't care, even though I know he does. The haphazard look works for him.

"You still hanging out with Hayley?" I ask.

He shrugs, turning his head a little. "Sometimes."

Ha. Sometimes. I guess that means whenever she gets a text from him.

"Farmer, let's go," Reid calls.

Cade fake bows to me and holds his hand out. I take it, and we walk out into the main locker room together. Both Reid and Lex are dressed more down than their friend, but they all look handsome. They always have been.

When we get to the parking lot, Cade turns toward his own vehicle. "I'm going to head out and pick Jules up. Meet you there."

He gets in his car, not leaving the rest of us with a chance to say anything. "Aren't we going to his camp?" I ask.

Reid shrugs. "He already gave the keys to a lower classmen on the team, telling him to get things set up." He opens the passenger door for me, and I scoot in.

Lex gets in next with Reid walking around the front of the car to get in the driver's side. As soon as Reid gets in, Lex asks, "Are you going to talk to him or should I?"

"Cade?" Reid asks.

I look between the two of them while they share a look in the rearview mirror. "What's going on?"

Reid shakes his head, but Lex asks, "You haven't noticed?"

"Notice what?"

"Nothing," Reid says, but it sounds like bullshit to me.

"Now I really want to know what's going on," I press, looking between the two of them.

The corners of Lex's mouth tilt up. "Cade likes Jules."

My mouth drops. "No."

Lex smiles and nods. "Yep."

I look to Reid who confirms it with a nod.

"What the fuck? What? But Jules—" I stop where I was going with that train of thought because it was headed in a direction that isn't true. Jules isn't Brady's girlfriend anymore.

"Don't worry, Briar," Lex says, reaching out to squeeze the top of my shoulder. "Jules doesn't see him like that."

"Yet," Reid adds. This time, his lips do twist into a smile, but it's short-lived. What we overheard in that tiny room is really bothering him.

I sit back in my seat, holding my arms to myself. I don't know how I feel about this. Brady and Jules were the real deal. They loved each other. They—

But Cade is a good guy. *If* he likes her and she likes him back, who am I to say anything about it?

"Relax, Briar," Reid says. He puts his hand on my thigh and squeezes as he drives down the highway. "Jules is still grieving. This isn't anything that's going to happen for a long time. If ever."

That's true, I tell myself. Jules might not even like Cade like that even when she does want to move on after Brady. I take a deep breath and let all the mixed emotions about this scenario seep away. Jules will find someone. It's not like she's going to become a nun just because my brother died. Eventually, I'll have to see her with someone else, and when that time comes, I need to be the friend she is to me. I need to tell her it's okay. As long as he's a good guy, of course. I need to tell her this is what Brady would want. As long as the new guy isn't a douche. Brady wouldn't like that. As long as—

Sweet Jesus, just stop!

Reid sighs after looking over at me. "You just had to say something, didn't you, Lex?"

"Dude, I thought she already knew. It's obvious."

Reid just shakes his head. "Just forget we said anything, okay?"

Yeah, right.

Reid and Lex talk a little about the game the rest of the way to Cade's camp, but I don't utter a peep. When Reid parks the car in the long driveway and I get out, Lex moves next to me. "Hey, don't say anything to Cade about what I said, okay? And don't say anything to Jules either. All I wanted to do was warn him that it's probably too early to say anything to her. Something he already knows."

I look up. Lex has always been the most caring out

of the four. Always worried more about what other people thought than the rest. "I won't say anything to either of them," I promise. "I guess I just realized that someday Jules will be with someone else."

"It'll be hard," Lex says. "But you'll just have to reassure her." He shuffles his feet. "Listen, Briar, I hope you know I'm okay with you and Reid."

The hair on the back of my neck stands.

"It fucking hurts, but I get it. Okay? It'll never change how I feel about you both as friends just like when Jules finds someone, you'll be there for her, and I'm here for the both of you."

It's hard for me to look at Lex when he brings stuff like this up. I know it's my fault he even thought he had a chance, and that's what kills me.

"Don't say sorry," Lex says, his voice dipping low. "I'm just telling you that I care enough about you both to let you have what you want. You're happy with one another. It's obvious."

I bite my lip, searching for the right words, but they never come. I don't know if they ever will come. Instead, I reach out and squeeze his bicep. "I care about you, too, Lex."

"I know," he says.

Reid's car beeps as he locks it, and then he comes around the side of the car, waiting for the two of us, so we can all walk up the drive together. Inside, it's the same party, different venue. I feel better that it's at Cade's parents' camp, but other than that, everything is exactly like the other parties. The keg is in the kitchen. Plastic cups are everywhere. They're tipped over on the ground, strewn on any available flat surface, or in people's hands.

Shouts rise up when Reid walks in. Some guys from the football team walk up to him, most of them probably already half drunk, and greet him with warrior yells that make me laugh. Reid reaches behind him to grab my hand and brings me to his side after bro hugging all of them. "We're celebrating tonight, Briar. Cade already warded off rooms for the three of us to sleep in. No one's allowed in any of them until we decide to head upstairs."

I bite my lip. "I don't know if I can. What about my mom?"

He winks at me. "She thinks you're spending the night with Jules. Don't worry, I told her you needed a girls' night."

I shake my head at him. "You know, one day she's going to realize you're lying to her."

He turns and pulls my hands around his hips until we're flush together. "Don't you think she already knows? It's just easier for her to pretend we're not at

Cade's parents' camp sleeping in the same bed together."

I tilt my head to the side. I'm guessing he's right. She did tell me she never wanted to walk in on us, and that probably means she doesn't want to have any possible moments thrown in her face either.

"I mean, your mom was once young too…"

I slap him on the shoulder. "Okay, that's enough of that talk." He leans forward and nibbles on my neck until I playfully push him away.

When Jules gets there, we dance all night while the guys play drinking games and get tipsy. Neither Sasha nor Oscar show up, which is a good thing because a drunk Reid will speak his mind even more than a sober Reid. Around midnight, he puts his arm around me while I'm on the dance floor. We dance two songs together before he pulls me up the stairs to the off-limits area to all party guests except us. "I've been watching you dance all night," he says.

"No, you haven't," I tease. "You've been playing beer pong."

"Okay, I've been playing beer pong *and* watching you dance all night. I can do two things at once, you know."

We move into the room farthest down the hall. I turn and stop in my tracks, my eyes bugging out at what I see on the bed. Reid closes and locks the door behind us, and when he turns, he almost plows into me. I'm staring at the bed, shaking my head and trying not to laugh.

"What the...?"

"Oh my God," I say.

Cade's put rose petals on the bed. I know it's Cade because in the middle of the soft brown comforter, there's a handwritten note that says, *Have fun, kids. Wash the sheets in the morning.*

"That motherfucker," Reid says, laughing. It starts out as a small laugh, but it grows from there like a snowball moving downhill. Before I know it, Reid's doubled over laughing. Something I haven't seen him do in a long time.

I help him over to the bed, make him sit, and then sit in his lap. He wraps his arms around me. "I'm glad we're here together."

"I'm glad you're smiling like that," I say. These past few weeks have been stressful. To see him having fun means so much to me. But, there's still the problem of what we heard in the supply closet. It affected him. I know it did. "After we overheard Coach and Oscar, I thought you were going to be miserable all night."

A shadow passes over Reid's face. He looks away

immediately, making my stomach churn. His arms grow stiff, and it's like he's turned cold, too.

So, I'm definitely not imagining things. "What is it, Reid? Do you know what Oscar meant by that?"

Reid sighs. "Yes."

"Well, care to share?"

Reid sets me on the bed next to him and moves away. "Not really because you're going to be mad."

My mind goes everywhere and nowhere all at once. It keeps trying to come up with a reason for why I would be mad about what he's going to say, but it keeps coming up with nothing. What could I be mad about? He's got everything going for him right now.

Reid clamps his hands together in front of him and his leg starts jumping up and down. The carefree guy who had a little too much to drink tonight is long gone. "What is it, Reid?"

His jaw hardens. "The note from my doctor? I faked it." His smile is evil, cocky, and laced with guilt all at the same time.

"Reid," I gasp.

He pushes himself off the bed and starts to pace. "You want to know why I faked it? I can't stand not having football. I feel one-hundred percent fine, and that doctor kept dicking me around for no reason. 'Next time, champ,'" he says, imitating the doctor's voice. "'We don't want you to get hurt, do we?' Christ, I was going crazy, Briar. Fucking crazy. I'm fine. Look what I just did out there. I played the best game I ever have. Tell me I'm not ready to play."

He continues to pace, simmering in his own anger. When he's done getting his secret off his chest, I stand. My arms are shaking I'm so angry, and his fury over the situation is only making me madder. "What if you'd gotten hit? What then, huh? What if you hit your head? You had a fucking concussion!"

"That's right!" he shouts back. "I *had* a fucking concussion. I don't have one anymore."

"So you say."

"So what?" he growls. "I know my body. I don't care what that doctor has to say, it's past time I came back. Fucking Drego out on the field taking my place, trying to steal my rewards." He shakes his head. "I couldn't let it go on any longer."

I take a deep breath. "But what if you were hurt? Would any of that matter?" I ask, my voice tiny even to my own ears. I'm not mad at Reid, not really. I get it, but the fear of losing him is popping into my head again.

Reid makes me sit and then drops to his knees in front of me. "I'd never do anything to take this away," he says. "I'm telling you I'm ready to be back out there. I know it."

I shake my head. "But what if you're not?"

"I am," he says. His green eyes lock with mine. We hold one another's gaze for a long time. I can tell he truly believes he's fine. I can tell he truly feels it right down to the marrow of his bones, and I want to believe him, too. I want to believe it the same way, but the doctor... He wouldn't have just lied. Reid runs a frustrated hand through his hair. "You're missing something in all this, Briar. If I'm the only one who knows I faked that doctor's note about coming back to play, how does Oscar suspect anything? How does he know something's up unless he was certain I wasn't coming back?"

I blink. I'm seriously grateful I didn't drink tonight because my brain probably wouldn't have been able to make the connection. "Sasha."

Reid slowly nods.

"But how? She can't control your doctor. That's crazy."

Reid shakes his head. "I thought the same thing, but Briar, it fits. It all fits."

My stomach bottoms out as I realize he's right. I don't know how she did it, but she did do it. She not only took Reid out, but she kept him out. Otherwise, how would Oscar know to question his return to playing story?

"Do you think Coach will look into it?"

Reid shakes his head. "No, only because he'd rather have me playing than not."

"And you didn't tell the guys?"

Reid's gaze shifts to the floor. His shoulders deflate like he'd been carrying this around with him. "No, I didn't tell them. I was afraid they wouldn't let me do it."

I slap his shoulder, anger seeping back in. "Well, they probably wouldn't have, jackass. Because we all care about you. You shouldn't be taking risks like this."

"Still care about me?" Reid asks, his green eyes slicing to mine. "Even though I kept this from you?"

"Well, of course. Even if I think what you did was brash and unreasonable. Not to mention hedonistic, cocky, and selfish, I—."

Reid doesn't let me get the rest of it out. He leans over and kisses me, stopping my tirade abruptly. I'm upset he would take his health into his own hands by forging a doctor's signature, but I can't seem to think about that at the moment. His kisses are fierce and strong. He moves me onto my back before following after me, his knees moving to either side of my hips. His tongue dives into my mouth like a man starved, and I open for him, giving him everything I have to give.

He takes my arms and pins them above my head. My skin glides across velvety rose petals until he holds me there. His free hand slips under my shirt before he takes a handful of my breast for his own. "You're wearing too many clothes." He pulls at the hem of my shirt until it slips past my arms and disappears somewhere to the side of us.

He presses his lower half into mine, and I moan when I feel his hard length press right where I need it. I'm only wearing thin leggings, so the barrier is nothing. I work on his jeans, unbuttoning the clasp and pulling the zipper down before he has to help me slip them over his legs. When he settles back on top of me, I move my hips into his, asking for it. Hell, practically begging for it.

Reaching around my back, Reid unclasps my bra and gently pulls the straps down my shoulders, revealing the swell of my breasts little-by-little as if he wants to tease himself. He's definitely teasing me. The fabric slips over my erect nipple, and when he finally does pull it away fully, he puts his hot mouth on my waiting skin, making me buck off the bed and into his hard body. He slips his hands under my ass as he continues to lavish my breasts, first one then the other.

When his hands reach the hem of my leggings, he pulls down, taking my panties with him until he's peeling off the fabric down my knees and past my ankles.

He stares at me for a moment, leaning back. His breath hits the wet area of my breasts from his kisses, sending a spark through me. "Now look who's wearing too many clothes," I say.

He yanks his shirt off, throwing it to the side until he's leaning over me, bulging out of his boxer briefs. I wrap my leg around his ass and pull him down until he's nestled at my entrance. He groans, arching into me. "I would never risk this, Briar. I swear," he says again, echoing what he said to me a few minutes ago. I know he's right. I know he wouldn't willingly do anything like that. "I want you to come to Warner's with me," he says, lifting his hips into mine.

I move my knees to the mattress, giving him access. His green eyes are molten. The self-confident Reid is back. He's sure again. Confident that all his dreams are going to come true. He's going to win the All-State Scholarship. He's going to Warner's. And I'm going to be there with him.

"Start a life with me," he says.

My breath catches. He stares into my eyes as he moves his boxer briefs down, releasing his dick from the confinement of his clothes. There are questions in his eyes, but when I lift my hips to his, telling him it's alright, he swallows. No condom this time. I feel him at my entrance first, then the slow, agonizing torture as he pushes inside me. I pull in a shaky breath, relishing the skin-on-skin contact. It's too perfect.

When he's fully inside, he rests his forehead on mine and continues to move inside me. My hips move up to meet his time and time again as we slowly pleasure each other like the greatest tease. He keeps his gaze locked on mine. It's as if he's trying to tell me that this is about me and him. It's not just about the act of sex. It's about having it with me and only me.

My body breaks out in goosebumps. "I love you," I say.

He closes his eyes briefly, then opens them again. "I love you." He moves onto his hands, using the angle of his body to slide deeper inside me, this time with a little more force. The bed moves, and I grip his hips, sliding my hands over his taut muscles. Soon, he starts to shake. Seeing him start to lose it makes the heat in my core ramp up. The pressure inside me builds. I move against him more fervently, and he does the same until he's rocking the bed in time with his thrusts inside me. "Fuck, Briar. Yes."

He grinds down onto me, and my body plunges into an orgasm. I call out his name, clinging to his hips as he rides my orgasm out and right into his own. His thrusts slow, like he's trying to make it last, but eventually, he drops to his elbows again, kissing me solidly on the mouth. He moves to his side and holds me to him, running his hands through my hair gently until I fall asleep.

He better be right about his health because I cannot lose this.

24

The next Monday at school, Oscar doesn't show. I notice in English that he isn't there, and I happen to catch a conversation between two girls lamenting the fact that he wasn't in one of their classes either. It seems like everyone else realizes he and Sasha aren't together anymore, too, so girls will be jumping all over him with his new available status.

When we woke the morning after the party, everyone else was gone except Lex and Cade. Reid told them what he'd done. I pushed him into it. He wanted to just tell them about what Oscar and Coach talked about, but I told him he couldn't do one without the other. They reacted the same way I did, especially Lex. His nostrils flared, and although he sat and listened to what Reid had to say after that, I'm not sure the issue is resolved between them yet.

Cade smirks across from Reid at the lunch table. "If he doesn't show up for school, he can't practice. I didn't think he'd quit. I thought for sure he'd go with the offer Coach gave him. He probably thinks anything but quarterback is beneath him."

Lex shakes his head. "Coach gave him an opportunity. It's up to him to take it. Honestly, I didn't think he was this stupid. This would still allow him a spot on one of the best teams in the state. He'll still get scouts. And, he's still up for the All-State, so what's the deal? He can't go back to Rawley Heights. Not that he'd want to, but besides that, every other team in the state has a quarterback. We're in the latter part of the season. Unless he wants to do some major digging to see which teams got a quarterback who sucks, he's stuck."

"Not to mention that Sasha put his family up in a townhouse here and got his mother a job. I'm not sure they can just leave now."

Cade's gaze narrows. "If Sasha's done with Oscar, you can bet their asses are already out of that fucking townhouse."

I hadn't thought of that. Shit. What if Oscar isn't here because he literally has no place to live?

"You feel bad for him, don't you?" Lex asks.

I press my lips together. I can feel the heat of Reid's gaze on me as I think about choosing the perfect words. "I know he's an asshole. There's probably no changing that, but I just can't help but think that if he'd grown up here, he would be a different guy."

"He'd still be an asshole," Cade says. His gaze moves to Jules' empty chair. She isn't at lunch because she's studying in the library for a History test, but I can tell he wishes she was.

"I don't deny that. You guys are assholes too."

"Hey," Lex says, looking truly injured.

I give him a look. The three of them know what they're like. I don't need to explain it to them.

One of the guys on the D-line comes over, clapping Reid on the shoulder. "Shit. Did you guys hear about Drego?"

My back straightens as I look over my shoulder at the guy.

"No. What?" Lex asks.

"Jumped," the guy says, his eyes widening. "Probably from those same dudes who were out front of the school that day. That shit must've sucked. They—."

"Is he okay?" I ask, interrupting him.

Reid stiffens next to me.

The guy shrugs. "In the hospital last I heard.

Trumbly talks to him." The guy motions with his head toward another football table. I follow his gesture to see Joe Trumbly, a senior. He's been a staple on the team even though he's not as good as most of the guys. He's decent, however, not good enough to play college ball by any means.

Lex stands from the table. "I'm going to get the scoop."

Cade sighs, looking from me to Reid, then follows after him.

Reid looks over his shoulder. "Thanks for letting us know, man."

The guy claps him on the shoulder again and goes to sit down with his tray of food. Reid immediately turns to me, his expression stormy.

I lower my gaze from the accusations in his eyes. "What?"

"I don't like the idea of you feeling bad for Drego. He's a punk."

"I didn't say he wasn't. Maybe I'm just being naïve, but he did help us," I remind him. "With Sasha."

"Yeah, only because it suited him. Think about it, Briar. He only helped because it didn't affect him. He already had my spot. He had Sasha. In some fucked up way of his, he thought what Sasha did was wrong, so he helped out in that respect, but do you think if I asked him to give me my spot back, he would? Do you think he wouldn't do something else that benefited him and fucked us over? Like he's already done to me?"

"No, I think he would do all that," I say, keeping my voice low even though Reid's rose. "I didn't say he was a good person. I just feel bad for where he grew up is all. That he had to worry about having a hard life. Which is obviously true since he just got jumped."

"He got what he deserved if you ask me," Reid says.

His green eyes are hard. I understand his feelings. I do. Oscar screwed him over, but if it wasn't Oscar, it would've been someone else. Sasha is the real culprit in all this. She would've just gotten another quarterback to come in. How? I have no idea, but she would go to any lengths to get Reid and me out of the way because we don't fit into her perfect life.

I've got news for her. Life isn't perfect. Life is messy and sad and fucked up at times.

But it can also be beautiful and hopeful.

———

"I can't believe you talked me into bringing you here. Reid's going to be so pissed."

I stare up at the white-washed walls of the hospital's exterior from within Jules's car. Lex found out what hospital Drego was in and now we're here. Well, I'm here. Jules is here under duress. "He'll live," I tell her. Seriously. If the man can forge a fucking doctor's note and not really know if he's okay, I can go visit a douche in a hospital. I just need to see that he's okay. "You'll wait here?" I ask.

She nods, her body stiff.

I get out of the car on shaky legs. I don't fully understand why I wanted to come here. It just feels like the right thing to do. So, instead of turning around, I forge ahead. I push open the glass doors and go right to the nurse's station to ask where Oscar's room is. They don't ask me if I'm a relative, so I take that as good news. If he was in ICU, they only let family visit. I would've lied, but that would only go so far if his mom was in the room with him when I came in and started asking who I was.

Instead, I take the elevator up to the second floor and turn right per the nurse's instructions. Three doors down on the left, I hesitate outside the right room number. Inside, I can hear a TV playing, but no other noises. I take a deep breath and push the door open. Without looking for him, I turn, closing the door behind me. It's really just to stall before having to come face-to-face with Oscar. It closes with a soft click. I shut my eyes, gather up the courage, and turn. He's probably going to think I'm nuts for coming to visit him.

When I lift my gaze, he's already staring at me. His eyelids narrow over dark irises as he waits for me to approach his bed. He's bruised. His lip is cracked. His left eye is swollen, and he's in a cast. I breathe out. So much for being a wide receiver. Oscar Drego's football season is fucked.

"You're probably wondering what I'm doing here," I say. My voice sounds small in the empty, barren room.

"Unless you're going to confess your undying love to me, I probably don't care."

I roll my eyes, and Oscar smirks, then grimaces, then tries to keep his face impassive like smiling didn't just hurt his face.

"We heard at school about what happened. Was it those guys from the Heights?"

Oscar looks away. He swallows. "Mom and I had to move in with my grandparents last night...in the Heights. Sasha kicked us out of the place we were staying in."

I'd already suspected as much, but a swell of anger grows bigger inside me. She knew what would happen to Oscar if he had to go back to the Heights.

"I can tell by your face," Oscar says. He shakes his head. "Yes, Sasha Pontine is a terrible fucking person. I'm just not sure I'm any better than her."

Can't argue with him there. "You going to be okay?" I ask.

"My football season's over." He lifts his casted hand gingerly. "They got me with a bat. The baseball bat is my thing, so of course they used it against me." He pauses for a second. "Some broken ribs. A fractured toe."

"Where's your mom?" I ask, looking around the small room to see if I can find any signs of her. Surely she's been here, right?

"She has to work, Briar. Luckily, they hired her back at the tiny shop down the street from my grandparents' house. No money equals no food."

"Has she been here at all?"

"She brought me here," he says, his tone defensive.

"I'm sorry. I didn't mean to imply—"

"People like you never do. You with your perfect families. You never understand what it's like to not have that."

I grind my teeth together. Maybe I would've agreed with him before, but it's not like I'm ever the innocent like he says. "You keep saying that, but you also keep forgetting I've been through shit, too."

His face loses some of its edge. "Coach offered your brother's spot to me."

"Were you going to?" I ask. Something I've been dying to know. It's obvious he's not going to be able to now, but I wonder if he was ever thinking about it.

"I always look out for me. Do you even have to ask that question?"

"I'm just curious if you were going to do something to Reid to get the quarterback spot. You know, finish what Sasha started. You wouldn't have to settle for wide receiver if you did."

He blinks and looks taken aback. "I told you I would never hurt you."

I take in a breath. Jesus. Oscar Drego is a conundrum wrapped in question marks. Does he even know why he does the things he does? "How'd you know Reid's letter was a fake?"

His eyes widen, then they return to normal a second later. "You were in the supply closet, huh? Thought about taking Sasha in there myself."

My cheeks pink, but I don't confirm his suspicions. "How'd you know, Oscar?"

"I'm surprised Reid told you he faked it. I didn't think he would since you were going to be pissed about it."

"I was—am pissed."

He looks me over. I realize I'm still standing in the exact same spot as when I first came in, hands clutched in front of me. I look around and spy a chair in the corner, so I slide it over and sit in it, raising my eyebrows to tell him I'm not going to let my question go, so he might as well answer it.

"I keep telling you to think bigger when it comes to Sasha. That same advice still stands."

"Don't talk around it, Oscar. How'd you know he forged the note?"

He laughs, the tone harsh, making me snap my head back. "You think I want to get involved in this anymore than I already am? Hell, we already lost our place to live. I got the shit kicked out of me. Now you want me to fuck with the big boys. No, not happening. I value myself above everything else, remember?"

I watch his face. When he looks away under my scrutiny, I realize he's afraid. At least a little. "I don't want to put you in any more danger," I tell him. "I'm not like you."

He winces. When he turns his gaze back on me, he looks sad. He looks like he doesn't have any hope left. I can't blame him. He's in the hospital all busted up. His football season is over. He and his mom don't have a place to live anymore, and she also doesn't have the job Mr. Pontine gave her either. Basically, most everything has been taken away from him and his family. I guess that's what you get when you're in league with Sasha.

"At least you're done with the situation now," I tell him. "You don't have to buddy up to Sasha anymore, and you could get away from the Heights."

"There aren't many options for poor people, Briar."

I feel so small at that moment, like how I felt when Brady got taken away. I actually have very little power at all. I couldn't help my dying brother. I can't help people like Oscar who live in poverty and run with bad people. He's right. How would he get out?

I stand, suddenly feeling awkward. I don't know what to say to him, and it's clear he doesn't know what to say to me. "Bye, Oscar," I say after we just stare at each other for a few seconds.

I turn to leave, but he calls out, "Hey, Briar?"

Slowly, I face him again. "Yeah?"

"I hope everything works out for you," he says, and he sounds almost genuine.

"I hope the same for you, too, Oscar. I hope you heal quickly, and no matter where you play football next year, I'm sure you'll kill it." Satisfied, I turn and start to leave. I didn't get what I came here for. I guess. Part of me was hoping he'd tell me what I feel like I'm missing with Sasha. The other part of me—the part that feels bad for him—wanted to help him, but I failed at both.

When I get to the door, I turn around one last time. "My parents own an insurance company. Sometimes they need extra people to file and do basic paperwork. If you or your mom ever get desperate, I can put in a good word for you. I can't promise anything, but..." I shrug, leaving the offer like that. He won't take it. He's got too much pride for that.

He nods, and we lock gazes one more time before I leave.

I'm pretty sure that's the last time I'll ever see Oscar Drego. And I can't say that I'm sad about it either.

25

Mom, Dad, and I are just sitting down to dinner when the doorbell rings. They all look at me since the only person who comes over anymore is Reid. I shrug, but get up anyway. When I look through the peephole, Reid's standing there with a big smile. Like a coward, I texted him earlier that I went to visit Oscar in the hospital and have yet to get a response back.

I open the door hesitantly. "Hey."

His grin widens, and he moves forward, picks me up, and holds me in the air for a moment. "I'm on the short list for the All-State Scholarship."

I gasp. "No way. That's awesome!"

He lets me slip back down to my feet. Behind us, my mom calls out, "Reid, is that you?"

"It is," he says.

He takes my hand after shutting the door behind him and practically leads me into the dining room. "Well, you look happy," she says, greeting him.

"I'm on the short list for the All-State Scholarship," Reid tells them. He can't keep the grin off his face, and the words come out in a burst like he can't contain them inside.

My mom grins, her eyes welling. Once upon a time, Brady wanted the same scholarship. My dad stands, holds out his hand, and shakes Reid's heartily. "That's great, Reid. Excellent news. I'll be shocked if they don't pick you."

Mom quickly agrees. Her tearful reaction isn't a response to seeing Reid make the list, it's to seeing a life Brady wanted go unlived. I know because I feel it right now, too. I drop Reid's hand and walk toward Mom, putting my hand around her waist and squeezing. "He would've wanted this for Reid."

"I know," she says, chastising me with a forced smile. "Of course, he would." She looks up. "Why don't you stay for dinner? We were just sitting down."

Reid agrees, and my mom leaves the room to get another place setting for him. Dad and Reid keep up the conversation regarding the All-State Scholarship, my dad asking who's won it in previous years and Reid answering with every single player except one. They had to look up that year. Finally, Reid turns to me. "Oscar made it on the short list, too."

My eyebrows rise. "Oh, yeah?" I hadn't even thought to ask. After I left his hospital earlier, I didn't expect to hear anything about him ever again.

Reid nods.

"I don't think it matters," I tell him. "You're going to win."

Reid shrugs. "He's a good player." His gaze locks on mine like he's trying to say something else with his words.

"Well, he won't be for the rest of the season. His arm is broken."

My mom gasps. "No. That's terrible." My mom has no idea who Oscar is, but she just can't stand to hear when people are hurt. I guess I have a bit of that in me, too. "What happened?"

I freeze. I don't really want to tell my parents he got jumped.

Reid must sense my hesitation because he says, "I think he fell. I don't know. An accident of some kind."

"Ugh," my mom says, clutching her chest. "That's just terrible. Poor kid. And at the end of the season too."

"He still has next year," I say, trying to lighten the mood.

"Who else is on the short list?" Dad asks Reid.

They throw out a few more names I recognize. Mostly big shot football players from surrounding towns. When dinner ends, I lead Reid back to my bedroom, keeping the bedroom door open after another reminder from my mother.

"Your mom's in denial," Reid whispers. I laugh, and he comes closer, gripping my hands in his. "You want to talk about visiting Oscar in the hospital?"

"Do you want me to talk to you about it?" I ask, still feeling uncertain.

He nods. "You're just like your mother. I should've known you'd feel sorry for him."

"It's not about liking him," I say.

"Please," he says, like that was the last thing on his mind. "I know."

I smile. "Good."

"So?"

I sit back on the bed and cross my feet in front of me. "He's pretty banged up. He wouldn't tell me who did it, but please, we know it was ex-teammates from the Heights. He said they did it with a baseball bat. Bruised, swollen face. Cracked lips. Broken arm. Broken ribs. Fractured toe."

Reid makes a face. "I bet he was livid."

"I don't know," I say, thinking back on our conversation. "He seemed...hopeless." I nod. "That's definitely the word I'd use. He just looked like there was nothing he could do." We're both silent for a little while. I don't expect Reid to say anything because I'm not going to change his mind about Oscar, and I don't even want to. "I asked him how he knew about your note."

Reid turns toward me with raised eyebrows. "What did he say?"

I shrug. "He didn't give me much, but he acted scared. Like he wanted to tell me, but it wasn't in his best interest to tell me either. He just told me to think bigger than Sasha."

"I agree," Reid says. "I don't think Sasha has the ability to know about my doctor's appointments, but it doesn't matter right now, anyway. She cornered me after practice."

"You're kidding."

He shakes his head. "She told me she knows my note's a fake. I told her I have evidence she was the one who paid Eli to sack me, so if she tells everyone about the note, I'll tell everyone about her mission to get rid of me."

I shake my head. This all sounds so cloak and

dagger. Why can't high school just be about first boyfriends and homework?

Then again, I don't have it as bad as some people do. At least I have a nice house, plenty of food to come home to, and don't have to worry about getting my ass kicked.

"You think it worked?"

"It better. She tried to act like she didn't care, but I don't believe her. I saw a flash of fear in her eyes. She wanted to see what I had, but I didn't show it to her."

"She's probably going right to Eli."

"No doubt," Reid says. "He won't be happy to see her."

"Who is?"

―――――

Reid picks me up like usual before school. He gets to my house in enough time for Mom to make him breakfast, which I think she secretly loves doing. When we get to school, Cade and Lex are already there. But that's not all, Sasha is leaning against the school in front of them, acting like she owns the place.

"What the hell is this?"

I groan inwardly. Cade and Lex wouldn't be talking to her for no reason.

Reid parks the car and then waits for me in front of it, so we can walk toward the school together. Lex gives him an apologetic look when we get closer. "Hi, Babe," she smiles, her eyes practically twinkling at Reid when we look up.

I'm used to her games, so I don't even let her words faze me. She's just delusional, and I know Reid wouldn't touch her with a ten-foot pole, so it's easier to tell myself she doesn't have a chance.

"What do you want?" Reid asks, his voice bored.

"Oh, I was just thinking about the conversation we had yesterday." She kicks off the school. "The one where you tried to threaten me?"

"The one where you tried to threaten me first?" Reid counters.

Sasha rolls her eyes. "You used to like it when I played games." She gives me a dirty once-over. "Now you're just a stick-in-the-mud."

"Leave Briar out of this."

"Gladly. Why don't you shoo along, Briar? Adults are talking."

I lift my hand to flip her off. What I really want to do is put my fist through her face. She doesn't care what she does to hurt people. First Reid. Then Oscar. She walks over people like they're shit, and she's the queen. "I think I'm fine right where I am." I smile at her, and the guys close ranks around me.

She acts like it doesn't bother her, but I see the tiny wrinkles near her eyes. "We have a problem, Reid. Kind of like that time when you couldn't stop fucking me when my parents were in the next room." She sighs like it was the best moment of her life.

I grit my teeth.

"Except this is a messier problem. I know your doctor's note is forged."

"So you told me," Reid says, choosing his words carefully.

"I'll be forced to tell everyone if you don't do it first."

"Why? You got another quarterback in your back pocket?" I ask.

"Ahh, Oscar," she says. "He was getting annoying, wasn't he?"

I want to rip her a new one. Tell her what Oscar looked like in the hospital. Tell her he's out the rest of this season because of her actions, but I know yelling at her about these things won't do any good. She literally has no moral compass. Reid said before she got it from her parents, which is crazy. Parents are supposed to teach their children what's right and wrong, not the other way around.

"I bet you hated him," she says, toying with Reid. "He took your spot after all."

"The only thing that annoyed me about Oscar was him hitting on my girl. Seems I'm not the only one who prefers Briar over you."

Sasha's eyes narrow dangerously. I really don't like the look in her eyes, but that doesn't keep me from smiling at what Reid's said.

"You didn't answer my question. Why do you care if Reid is quarterback? I doubt you have another one to take his place."

"I don't give a fuck who takes his place," she snarls. "I just want him gone." She breathes for a few seconds and smooths her voice out. It's literally like she composed herself in a span of a few seconds. She looks at Reid. "It's not fair you're coming back under false pretenses."

"But it's fair that you took me out?"

Her lips tip up. "What happened to you was an accident. Anyone saying otherwise is delusional. If Eli's the one who told you this falsehood about me, he was just jealous that I chose Oscar over him. It's sad you got caught up in his revenge, Reid. You used to be so much smarter."

Cade crosses his arms over his chest. "Are you going to tell us why you brought us over here or not?"

She winks at him. Disgusting. Like hell Cade would touch her after what she's done. That's just sad.

"I just came to give my ex-boyfriend a friendly warning. I know the note's forged, and I'm prepared to tell Coach about it. I doubt you'll be playing in the next game, which is a shame since I hear scouts from Warner's will be there. That's still your dream school, right? It would be so sad if you didn't get this figured out by then."

Reid's muscles bunch. He breathes heavily out his nose, but instead of giving into her, he turns, kisses me on the temple, and says, "Thanks for letting me know."

We start to walk away, but Sasha stops us with a cat-like hiss. "Reid, you better fucking take this seriously because I will do it."

"And just how would you know this information, Sasha?" Reid asks, spinning around. "Are you fucking my doctor?"

She moves forward, hand raised like she's going to slap him, but Lex easily plucks her wrist from the air and moves it down to her side while she fights against him the whole time. "You asshole."

He shrugs. "I'm just wondering how you know my medical information. Seems odd, doesn't it? We'll see who does what with what," he says, then he turns, taking my hand again as we walk into school.

My mind starts running with every possible scenario.

"Shit. Do you think Warner's scouts are really going to be at the next game?" Cade asks when he comes up behind us.

"I wouldn't doubt it," Reid says. "Her father is in the habit of knowing just about everyone and everything. It's possible he found out the scouts are coming."

"Take it to Coach," Lex says. "Hell, I'll take it to Coach. I'll ask him if the scouts are going to be there or if Sasha's just trying to get at you."

"Either way," I speak up. "We have to believe that she's going to tell Coach Reid's not cleared to compete. Whether the scouts are there or not, he'll have to take him off the team again."

Reid squeezes my hand. "It'll be fine."

He stares down at me, but his facial expression, his eyes, and his words are all saying different things. He's worried. Sasha's just that stupid to do something when she knows we have something on her. I guess it's go down but go down swinging. If her parents are as powerful as they say, maybe she's not worried about the repercussions. She'll play the victim. The evidence we got is good, but it's her word against Eli's, and I know Sasha is one hell of a liar. In fact, she's banking on it. It'll be just like when she catfished me and spread around the picture of my breast. She'll get a slap on the wrist, and that's it.

I can't let her do that again. Not to Reid.

26

I've been doing way better at school. My grades are back up to where they were before Brady was taken away from us too early. But for the next few days as Friday night's game looms in front of us, I haven't been able to think about anything other than what Sasha's going to do to Reid, and how I have to figure out a way to stop it.

Reid's back in denial mode. He doesn't think she'll do what she says she's going to do, but I see the way she looks at him in the hallway and in the lunchroom. She's looking at him as if she's the predator, and he's the prey. She truly thinks she's unstoppable. No matter how many times I try to bring it up to Reid, he tells me it'll be fine and that he doesn't want me involved in any of it.

That same day Sasha threatened him, though, Coach pulled Reid and the guys aside and confirmed the fact the Warner's scouts are going to be there for the next game. To me, that brings more credence to what she told us in front of the school. Reid's been the opposite. He's been completely distracted by football ever since, but I'm so afraid he's preparing to smash this one game and he won't even have the opportunity to play. Aside from following her around and making sure she never gets an audience with Coach or anyone else important, I don't know what to do.

Actually, that's a lie. I have an idea. I just think it's crazy and that I won't be able to pull it off.

So, when Friday rolls around, I sit on the edge of my bed dressed for school and chew on my thumb knuckle, staring down at my phone. I pick it up and go to the text thread Reid and I have. I close my eyes. I have to talk myself into doing this. I know Reid would do the same thing for me, but I'm about to threaten an adult, a doctor no less, so I'd be worried if I didn't have a little apprehension. **Don't come pick me up. Jules is going to. She needs some girl time with me. We might be late.**

There are a couple of problems with what I've just sent him. One, Jules doesn't even know she's picking me up yet. Two, we don't need girl time. I know I'm lying to him right now, but since it's for his own good, that makes it better, right?

OK. Be safe.

I take a deep breath and get out of that text conversation as soon as I can. I go right to Jules' name and hit the call button. She answers on the second ring. "Hey," I say to her.

"What's up?" she asks. Her voice is a little breathless like she's been running around. "Is everything okay? Did Sasha say something yet?" We finally had to fill her in on what Reid did, so she's been as worried as the rest of us.

Also, she's of the same mind as me. She thinks Sasha's definitely going to say something, damn the consequences. Reid even tried to get an appointment with another doctor to get checked over, but he couldn't make one in such short notice. Especially with the doctor not being acquainted with his past medical information.

"No," I say. "Not that I know of. But I have an idea about that. Something that might help."

She responds immediately. "Whatever it is, I'm all for it."

"Can you pick me up? I'll tell you about it on the way to where we're going."

"And I take it we're not going to school?"

"Nope. Not yet, anyway."

"Be right there," she says.

It's one of those mornings where both my parents had to go into the office early, which I'm grateful for. If I had to pretend like everything was fine right now, I couldn't. My mom would be able to see right through me. Fortunately, it doesn't take long for Jules to get here. I slide inside her car once she's put it in Park. She's already twisted in the seat toward me. "Okay, what's the plan?"

I rub my forehead. When I'm about to say it out loud, it sounds crazy. "I thought we'd pay Reid's doctor a visit."

"Okay," she says, like I've just told her my parents are cooking meatloaf tonight.

"Okay?"

Jules cracks a smile. "Briar, Reid and the guys were there for me after Brady died, too. I'm with you one-hundred percent. We can't let Sasha do this to Reid. It's not right. But, I think we need more of a plan than just go visiting him…"

I nod. "I thought we'd pose as friends of Sasha's. Tell him we want to know why he signed off on Reid's note. Hopefully," I say, pulling out my cell phone and showing her the recording app I downloaded last night and made sure I knew how to work this morning.

Thank you, Cade, for giving me the idea. "If he knows something about what happened, he'll talk. If he doesn't, no harm done." I don't tell her that I'm desperate. If it doesn't work, I'm threatening to expose everything. After Reid asked if Sasha if she was fucking his doctor, I'm convinced the doctor has to be involved somehow.

She nods slowly. "I like everything but the friends part. If they're involved in this together, the doctor would know if Sasha had siblings, so let's say cousins. That makes it more understandable as to why we would want to know."

"Agreed," I tell her. I sit back, reading the address to Reid's doctor's office off my phone, hoping to get there before any real patients show up, and also hoping that just Sasha Pontine's name will get us in the door.

We cross town in just shy of ten minutes. "Okay," Jules says as soon as we park. "Don't break with our story even if he gets mad."

My stomach clenches. "Why would he get mad?"

"I don't know. If he did what we're accusing him of, he could get in serious trouble. Don't come right out and say that he did it. Really play up the angle that we're cousins, and we want to know why he signed Reid's paperwork to return to playing."

"Got it," I tell her.

We step out of the car and walk in at the same time. I try to give myself that Pontine air of knowing everything and being in charge of everything. Basically, I put on my resting bitch face and approach the front desk. When I first talk, I hear my voice waver, but eventually it comes out surer. "Excuse me, I'm Lizzie and this is Jane. We're here to see Dr. Campbell about our cousin, Sasha Pontine."

"Do you have an appointment?" the lady asks. She's staring us down, and my breath hitches in my chest.

"No, but can you tell him it's important, please?"

"Have a seat," the woman says.

Jules and I move to two of the waiting room chairs. There's only one other person in the room, the tip of their nose bright red. I immediately pull out hand sanitizer and offer it to Jules. She waits until I'm looking at her and then smirks. "Lizzie and Jane, huh?"

"I panicked," I tell her. "I think I moved my copy of Pride and Prejudice last night, so those names were stuck in my head. You know I can draw a lot of similarities between Darcy and Reid."

Jules laughs despite the fact that we're in the middle of something we would never dream of doing. "How so?"

"Arrogant. Cocky."

"Handsome," Jules says, fluttering her eyelashes at me.

"Well, yeah. Duh."

"Girls," the nurse calls. "He'll see you now."

I start in my seat and then stand, Jules right behind me. She points down the hallway, and we go through a set of swinging doors. Once we're inside, I take my phone out and start the recording. I have no idea where I'm going, but I try to act like I do while the scent of alcohol hits my nostrils. Then, I see him. His door is ajar, and he has a nameplate at the front of his desk that says Dr. Campbell, so that was easy enough. We walk in. He looks up, and his expression is definitely on the unfriendly side. "Hello, Dr. Campbell," I say. "I'm Lizzie, this is Jane. We're Sasha Pontine's cousins."

"So my receptionist tells me." He leans back in his seat. "I have patients, you know. And I'm pretty sure you ladies should be at school."

"I promise we won't take up any more of your time than we need to. Sasha would be here herself, but she's busy," I tell him, trying to speak as clearly as I can. "She wants to know why you approved Reid Parker's return to football."

"Christ," the doctor mutters. He gets up and closes his door before turning on us. "I don't know what you're talking about, and I can't believe you're coming to my place of business to talk about this shit."

I swallow. I've never heard a doctor behave in such an unprofessional manner. Jules speaks up then. "Well, frankly, Doctor, Sasha can't believe you did what you did, so I guess we're all on the same page."

The doctor sighs. "I already told her..." he breathes out, then shuts his mouth. He returns to the other side of the desk, sits, and steeples his fingers in front of him. "Did your cousin tell you I already talked to her on the phone?"

"She did," I say. "That's why she sent us here. She doesn't believe you." I have no idea if what I'm saying is the wrong thing or the right thing, but I'm just trying to put myself in Sasha's shoes. If she had some sort of arrangement with the doctor that would keep Reid out of playing, she would be calling this guy out right now.

"I told her I'd call Mitch about this."

"Well, you must not have done that yet, which is why we're here."

"Jesus," the doctor says. "The trouble you've all gone through to get one kid out of playing football. It better—."

"Oh, it's worth it," I say. My insides jump. I'm practically screaming from the rooftop. This guy *was* in on this. Not only that, so was Mitch. Fucking Mr. Pontine.

"I told Sasha, and I'll tell Mitch when I talk to him. I did not sign that kid's return to athletics note. I told him I would keep him out, and I did. I kept him out. Even though the kid is as strong as an ox. He could've returned right away." He leans forward, resting his elbows on the desk in front of him, scattering some papers. "You know how much trouble I could get in for this? Why would I fuck it up by signing his damn return letter? I know the consequences."

I want to ask him what the consequences are. I want to ask him what the hell the Pontine's have over him, so he would do this despite the consequences, but if I'm really Lizzie, Sasha's cousin, I would know this already.

"More than likely, the kid forged the note, which is what I told your cousin when I talked to her. There's nothing I can do about that."

Jules turns toward me. She nods, her eyes widening a fraction. "I don't know, Lizzie. I think he's telling the truth."

"Me too," I say.

"We'll be sure to let our aunt and uncle know."

The doctor sighs. "Good. And tell them I'm not working with anymore kids. I'll deal directly with them next time." He gives us a disgusted look then returns to the paperwork on his desk, ending the meeting

Jules shrugs, and then we both stand and head for the door. Our footsteps increase as we walk down the hallway, the waiting room, and finally the outside before we make it to Jules's car. "Holy shit," she breathes as soon as we get inside.

"He kept him out," I say, still disbelieving that we actually got what we came here to get. I pull my phone out and stop the recording. For good measure, I go to the beginning and play it again, making sure everything can be heard.

When we listen to the whole thing again, Jules smiles. "We got him."

We do indeed.

27

We don't run to the school or to the guys right away. Jules leaves the doctor's parking lot and goes to a nearby playground to park while we talk things through. We come to a decision that we should take the recording to Coach first because we did this first and foremost for Reid. Then, we'll take it to the principal who might finally be able to do something about Sasha. He might not be able to do anything to her like the police can, but this started about high school, it should end about high school.

Sasha thinks she runs the school. If the principal gets out of this what we got out of it, she won't for much longer.

Once our plan is ironed out, we decide to head to Spring Hill High. Usually, slipping into school is harder than slipping out of school. Luckily, when we open the double doors and go in, no one's around to ask for a hall pass. We both make a beeline right for Coach's office and knock on it.

The look on his face when he hears the entirety of our conversation with Dr. Campbell is priceless. He taps his pen on the desk a few times when I stop the recording. He shakes his head. "And all I had to worry about at school was not letting my grades slip too low so I couldn't play football."

"So you believe us?" I ask.

"Informally, yes. Formally, no."

My brows pull together.

"Miss Page, your brother was a fine player. You're reminding me of him right now." He smiles and taps his pen on his desk again. "I'm going to get my own doctor out here to evaluate Reid. This is a big night for him. You know that. If he can be out there, I'm putting him out there no matter what. If the doctor I bring in says he can't, then there's nothing I can do. You of all people should respect the fact that I don't play with my players' health."

"Of course, Coach," I say. I look toward Jules. This is a good thing. That asshole Dr. Campbell said Reid was ready to play pretty much right after he was injured. I have no fear that he won't pass whatever test this doctor puts him through. "There's something else, too," I tell Coach.

"What's that?"

"There's nothing you can do about it probably, but we also have evidence that Sasha Pontine paid Eli Richards, the player who sacked Reid the night he got hurt, to hit him hard enough to hurt him. He even put extra weights in his pads," I say, motioning to my forearms.

"So, that was the noise?" Coach asks.

I blink at his reaction. It's the same one Lex had.

"I think if you have evidence to that fact, whoever has it should take it to the police, including what you have here. I know you came to me because you want to make it right for Reid, and I'm sure he's going to be grateful, but if someone is really scheming to hurt Reid Parker, the police should deal with it."

I nod, agreeing with him. They should deal with it, but just my luck, they'd deal with it like they dealt with my boob pic. I don't need to get into that detail with Coach Jackson, though, so I thank him for listening, and then Jules and I both march down to the principal's office.

Mr. Dade is a little harder to convince. I can see the doubt on his face, but Jules and I play the recording for him several times and show him the text message

Reid took a picture of between Sasha and Richards. After that, Mr. Dade calls in Ms. Lyons, the school counselor, and Miss Higgins, the cheerleading coach.

Ms. Lyons takes us from the room while Mr. Dade and Miss Higgins discuss what to do with Sasha. I also emailed Mr. Dade the audio file and text message pictures at his request before leaving his office.

When we're in the school counselor's office, I don't get the same vibe in here like I used to. It used to be a place that felt like another trap, another time someone wanted something from me. Even though Ms. Lyons only wanted to help me, I wasn't in the right space to be helped. Now, I am.

"I think we need to call the police," she says. "These are some serious accusations, girls, and although SHH will do what we can on our end, I think other action needs to be taken. I can call your parents, so you can talk with them to discuss it, but I strongly urge it."

Jules looks over at me. "It's up to you. Actually, it's up to Reid. This is about him."

"I agree," I say, biting my lip. I turn back to Ms. Lyons. "I have to talk to Reid about this, but I can't talk to him about it right now. He's got a big game tonight. The Warner's college scouts are going to be there. He can't deal with this right now."

Ms. Lyons nods slowly. "You tell Reid if he needs me to assist in any of this he can come see me whenever he wants."

I stand, hearing the last bell of the day sound overhead. We spent a lot more time in Mr. Dade's office than I thought. "Thank you, Ms. Lyons. You've always been a help to me."

She looks taken aback by my words, but recovers. She places her hand over mine on her desk. "You are a strong woman, that's for sure, Briar Page. I think you're going to come out the other side of this okay."

I thank Ms. Lyons again, and then Jules and I move into the waiting area. My phone vibrates, and I pull it out. "It's Reid," I say. I scan the text and look at Jules. "He wants to know where we are."

"Tell him I needed a day and that we'll be there for the game."

I nod, type all that out, and send it. Adding a few kiss emojis for good measure and telling him I can't wait to see him after he kicks ass tonight and makes the Warner's scouts cream their pants over his football skills.

I mean, that's my man. I have to say things like that.

Jules blows out a breath. "What do you think's going to happen next?"

"Who knows?" I sigh, hoping we did the right thing.

At SHH, though, it seems like pretty much anything is possible. Right now, the only thing I'm hopeful for is that Reid will be able to play in tonight's game.

28

When it comes time for the game, Jules and I exit the school and walk to the bleachers. People are already streaming in wearing our school colors and waving little flags. It seems like everyone is hyped tonight, and I doubt even half know there are scouts here to look at some players.

Jules and I tried to circle back around and find Coach earlier to figure out what his doctor said, but we couldn't find him. Hopefully, he's keeping Reid's head in the game and not what's going on around him. If he's even able to play at all.

As we're walking up the sidewalk, a figure moves in behind us, "Excuse me, bitches," she says, then pushes between Jules and me. I watch her blond hair flip back and forth in a ponytail and the skirt of her cheerleading uniform swish back and forth.

Jules and I stop walking right then and there, causing people to divert around us.

"What the fuck?" Jules hisses under her breath. "Is she seriously being allowed to cheer at the game tonight? After all that?"

Sasha turns, smiling glaringly white teeth. "Tell your boyfriend I say hi as they take him off the field," she calls back, waving at us.

I step forward, but Jules holds me back. "She doesn't know," Jules says, lowering her voice. "She has no idea." She points to the side of the school. "Look, here comes Miss Higgins."

Jules and I move closer, then watch as Miss Higgins intercepts Sasha near the entrance to the field.

We pull ourselves off the path and watch. It doesn't take long for a self-satisfied smirk to cross my face.

"What?" Sasha screams.

Miss Higgins looks around nervously and says something else under her breath.

Sasha doesn't even listen, she lets go on a tirade of epic proportions. "I'm the best cheerleader out there. Hell, I'm the best thing that ever happened to this school, you can't take me out. That's ridiculous."

Someone clears their throat behind us. Jules and I

turn to see Mr. Dade walking Mr. and Mrs. Pontine up the walk toward Sasha. We catch a snippet of what he's saying to them. "Like we discussed in my office, I'm going to have to enforce your daughter's immediate expulsion and barring from the grounds while the matter is looked into. If it's found unwarranted, she can come back to campus immediately."

"It will be found unwarranted," Mr. Pontine says in that same haughty tone his daughter has.

"Until then," Mr. Dade says, "there's nothing I can do."

"Come on, Sasha," Mrs. Pontine says as they get closer. Sasha looks over, her eyes bugging out of her head. Her mother gestures for her to come to them. "We're going."

Sasha's mouth drops. "No, Mom. This is the biggest game of the year. Plus, Mr. Dade," she says, finally seeing him. "Reid Parker is playing out there when he shouldn't be. His doctor's note was falsified. Ask Dr. Campbell."

"We're aware of the predicament Mr. Parker is in," Dade says casually. "A separate physician reviewed him before the game and approved him for play."

"What?" Sasha shrieks. Her voice must be going hoarse from all the squealing.

"Don't speak anymore," Mr. Pontine tells her,

pulling his daughter by the elbow. "We'll be in contact," he says over his shoulder to both Miss Higgins and Mr. Dade.

Sasha's face is flush. Her parents lead her away awkwardly. People have stopped to look at the scene, but as if by kismet, she happens to meet my eye. I wave and smile at her, wishing I could tell her she bit off more than she could chew.

She sneers at me and looks away, obviously taking the advice of her father and keeping her mouth shut.

Jules envelops me in a hug. "Holy shit. That just happened."

"I know," I say, barely able to believe it myself.

"And Reid was cleared!"

She takes my hand, and we run toward the stands together to get a good seat. This is one game we won't want to miss.

REID PLAYS THIS GAME EVEN BETTER THAN THE last. I scan the stands for the scouts, but don't recognize them, so instead, I spend every ounce of energy cheering him on. The cheerleading squad is a mess tonight, which makes me laugh. It seems like no one knows what to do when the queen bitch isn't around. Not even Miss Higgins.

As the clock ticks down, signaling the end of the game, I don't know how Reid could've done anything differently. If Warner's doesn't want him after this, they're blind. They're stupid. They're just plain morons.

Jules tries to slip away when the game ends, but I make her come stand with me by Brady's memorial as the team celebrates their victory. I'm not really doing it for me. I'm kind of doing it for Cade. If it were me who just had a hell of a game in front of a bunch of college scouts, I'd want the girl I liked to be there afterward.

I'm positive we won't see them until after they get out of the locker room, but I'm wrong about that. Jules nudges me, and I look up. Reid's running toward me, his helmet in his hand. There are two dark slashes under his eyes that help keep the sun at bay during his games, but they don't take away from how handsome he is. He runs right to me and doesn't stop. He drops his helmet and picks me up, holding me high in the air. After looking at me for a few moments, he pulls me to him. "I know what you did for me, Briar, and I'm never going to forget it."

He holds me like a man clinging to life. Like a man who will try everything in this life not to let me go.

I don't let him say anything more, I just kiss him. We kiss and kiss until Jules clears her throat. Actually, we kiss through that one too, but eventually, Lex clears his throat, and we finally break apart.

"Reid," Lex says. "This is Mr. Chapman. He's from Warner's."

Reid turns, almost dropping me on my ass. I don't think I've ever seen Reid's face turn red before, but I see it now. Mr. Chapman holds his hand out, so Reid shakes it. "Nice to meet you."

Coach is there, too, smiling. My whole body buzzes. "You got quite the team here, Coach Jackson," Mr. Chapman says, looking at all three of my friends.

"That I do."

"I think I'd like to talk to you about a few of your boys." He nods at Cade, Lex, and Reid in turn, calling them by their names.

Holy shit. This is happening. He must want all *of them.*

Coach says, "I think we can arrange that." They head back toward the front entrance to the school. To Coach's office, not the locker room. That has to be a good sign.

"Fucker," Cade says, punching him in the arm. "Chapman was looking for you."

Reid puts his arm around me. "I had to see my girl."

I don't know what else happens after that because all I see is Reid. His green eyes. The sweat still dripping from the tips of his hair. The quirk of his lips, and the way he looks at me like there's no chance on this earth there could ever be any other person for him than me.

And I happen to agree.

"I guess we're going to Warner's," he says, his eyes lighting.

"I guess we are," I mimic back.

He leans over, brushing his lips against my ear. "Forever."

"Forever," I say softly.

He puts his hand in mine, and we walk toward SHH. The place I tried like hell to get away from, only to find out it was the place that would change my life forever.

It turns out I don't have the Spring Hill blues anymore. Reid took care of that.

EPILOGUE

I walk out of Reid's parents' kitchen with two cups of hot chocolate, taking them to Reid in the informal living room while wearing just his shirt and nothing else. His parents are away on a business trip again, so we have the whole place to ourselves. These are my favorite times.

When I get closer, the reporter talking on the TV gets louder. "Dr. Campbell's Medical Associates office building was searched today after a subpoena was filed for medical records pertaining to one patient. The police haven't released particulars as the patient is a minor, but it seems to be a related case to the Mitch and Clare Pontine case we've been reporting about over the last several weeks. We don't yet know how the malpractice suit is related in conjunction with the

Pontine's alleged money laundering schemes and falsifying documents accusations. More tonight on the six o'clock news after the press conference with Sheriff Mills."

When the report cuts back to two news anchors sitting at a desk, I walk in. "What are you watching that for?" I ask, handing him the mug of cocoa I made him.

He smiles. "Because...it makes me feel like maybe there is a bit of justice in this world. By the way, Cade texted me this morning. Hayley told him the Pontine's are moving away from Spring Hill. There was a moving truck outside their place this morning."

"They can't leave the state, can they?" I ask.

He shakes his head. "I guess they're heading to Mrs. Pontine's sister who lives a couple of hours away. Up north."

I still can't believe how this thing blew up. Reid definitely did get his justice.

"Sooo," he says, patting the cushion next to him. "I've been wanting to talk to you about something."

I just look at him. I don't know if I can take any more surprises. I've had to talk to the police more than a few times, and Jules and I will definitely be called as witnesses in Dr. Campbell's case. At least, that's what the detectives tell us. They may not need us if they find enough evidence that he lied about Reid's condition at the behest of the Pontine's.

"It's not bad," he assures me.

I visibly relax. He places his cocoa down on the coffee table and then takes mine from me and puts it down next to his. "Our lawyer tell us that we're, at the very least, going to get a settlement from what's happened with the Pontine's."

"Really?"

He nods. "It's probably going to be a lot."

"That's great, Reid." I bite my lip, then stare at him open-mouthed. "You know what that means? Even if you don't get the All-State Scholarship, which you will, but even if you don't, you can go to Warner's. They've already recruited you." My heart fills. This is everything to Reid.

"That's not all," he says, taking my hand.

"Okay..."

"My parents said since this is all happening because of what someone did to me, I can do whatever I want with the settlement. Of course, school is number one. But I was also thinking..." His lips pull up, but he suddenly turns very serious. "I want to use some of the money to rent an apartment off campus at Warner's, and I want you to move in there with me."

I blink at him. I can't say I've never thought about

how much I already want to live with Reid. We're with each other all the time. Any spare moment. I had only ventured to guess that once we got to Warner's, we would have to stay in each other's dorm rooms if we wanted to spend time with one another, but this? This is something I thought we'd have to wait years for. "That would be amazing," I say simply.

"So, you'll move in with me?" he asks.

"God, yes," I tell him. "Of course. Were you really worried I'd say no?"

"No," he says, taking my face in his hands. He moves a stray piece of hair out of my eyes. "Only because I see the same feelings I have for you reflected back at me."

And there's my big, burly football player being all sentimental again.

Reid Parker is the only one who could've brought me back from my grief over Brady. He's the only one who could've pushed me to bring my life back around to where it should've been headed. If not for myself, then for the life I want to live with him.

"I guess this is a good time to tell you that I killed the PSAT's. Even beat Theo Laughlin."

"Poor Theo," Reid says while dragging me onto his lap. "He doesn't realize he never had a chance." He holds my hips, smiling at me. "I knew you could do it, Briar. Brady's cheering you on from up there."

"He's cheering *both* of us on," I say, correcting him.

That's something I wholeheartedly believe. A notion I'll treasure for the rest of my life.

Correction: The rest of my life with Reid Parker.

The End

About the Author

E. M. Moore is a USA Today Bestselling author of Contemporary and Paranormal Romance. She's drawn to write within the teen and college-aged years where her characters get knocked on their asses, torn inside out, and put back together again by their first loves. Whether it's in a fantastical setting where human guards protect the creatures of the night or a realistic high school backdrop where social cliques rule the halls, the emotions are the same. Dark. Twisty. Angsty. Raw.

When Erin's not writing, you can find her dreaming up vacations for her family, watching murder mystery shows, or dancing in her kitchen while she pretends to cook.

Printed in Great Britain
by Amazon